Agent Arrow

G.A. Crisp

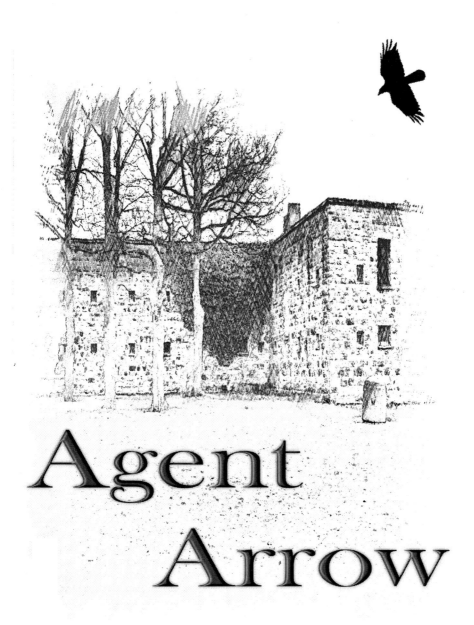

Agent Arrow

G. A. Crisp

Published in 2009 by Pigwidgeon Books

© Copyright 2009

Geoffrey Alan Crisp

A CIP catalogue record for this title is available from the British Library

ISBN 978-0-9562100-0-5

Pigwidgeon Books

36 King George VI Avenue,
East Tilbury,
Essex,
RM18 8SL.

A note from the author

      Thank you for buying my latest book. This is the third story that I have had the pleasure of writing, the first two, *"Night Stalker"* and *"Tom Fanshawe and the Apple blossom Ghost"*, have been well received and enjoyed by those that have read them.

      Once again, thank you for your support.

G. A. Crisp

Chapter One

Monty Barrington-Wright, stood at the top of the slope, by St. Mary's Church, looking down on the old fort, nestling in a natural depression, behind the river bank, on the Essex side of the Thames. Ever since he could remember, he had dreamed of owning the solid, granite block built, bastion. Now, finally, at the age of fifty three, he was within a hairs breadth of realising his boyhood dream. All it needed, was for the local authority to agree his plans, and it was his. Monty had spent months, in meeting after meeting, with his architects and the council, building department, discussing and fine tuning his plans. Looking down at the view that lay before him, he could now appreciate, exactly what they were protecting, and made a mental note, to write and thank them, for their time and effort.

His plan, was to turn the derelict fort, into a home with all the mod cons, that would make his life extremely comfortable, and no doubt, enviable to some people. In his mind, he could picture the landscaped gardens, that would replace the weed strewn mud, which surrounded the ancient monument. As a trade off with the council, Monty had agreed to build a park, for the use of the local community, as well as a wild life sanctuary, investing enough money into the project, so that it could keep going, until it became self supporting. In return, he would not only be allowed to convert the fort, into living accommodation, he had also been given permission, to turn the gun emplacement, that stood about three hundred yards away, from the main building, into a restaurant and the water tower, right on the river bank, into a tea room. Monty had in turn promised, to donate part of the profits, to local community projects.

Monty had already found the perfect place for his office. A spot which would give him uninterrupted views of the river and the surrounding flood planes, in both directions.

"All I need, is that permission" he thought to himself. Almost, as if on cue, his mobile phone gave a quiet warble.

'Hallo'?

'Is that Mr. Barrington-Wright'?

'Yes' Monty felt his stomach turn.

'Mr. Barrington-Wright, this is Vincent Peebles, from the planing office'

'Mr. Peebles, how are you'? Monty felt excited and nervous all at the same time. Almost as if in a visual display, of how his emotions where somersaulting, the knuckles of the hand holding the phone, turned white, as his grip tightened.

'Well, thank you' there was a short pause, then, Peebles spoke again 'I have some good news for you'

Monty, could almost hear the man's smile, in his voice

'Yes'? he answered breathlessly.

'We had a meeting this morning, and we have all agreed, to grant you, planning permission'

'YES! YES! YES!' shouted Monty, as he danced around in a circle, in the middle of the road 'She's mine'! he started to laugh. Then, at the top of his lungs, bellowed 'YEEEEES'!

'Hallo'? when no answer came, Peebles said again
'Hallo'?
'I'm sorry Mr. Peebles' he could hardly speak, let alone
think 'I was just doing a little dance'
'So I heard' at the other end, the council official was
wearing a big grin 'There are just a few small, but minor
alterations, that need to be taken into consideration, but
judging by our past meetings with you, I'm sure that
there will be no problems'
'None at all'
'So, will you pop in and see us, too discuss the changes'?
'Of course' he was breathing heavily, after his exertions
'Will tomorrow morning be ok'?
'That'll be fine. See you then'!
The line went dead.
Monty took a last long look at the fort. As he turned
away, he chuckled happily to himself.

Chapter Two

The minor alterations, were very minor indeed. After having them quickly sorted out, Monty started the job of getting quotations for the work that needed to be carried out. He also needed to find himself an experienced project manager, to run such an enormous enterprise.

After nearly three months had gone by, the contractors had all been chosen and the final plans made. Monty was walking around the grounds of the fort, with Harry "Duke" Elington, discussing the first phase of the refurbishment.

'Tomorrow morning, the roofers and the wrecking crew move in'! stopping for a moment, to look up at the massive granite wall, Duke scratched his head 'I've done some interesting jobs before, but never one as exciting as this one' he smiled at Monty, who returned his beaming look, with one of his own 'Anyway, as I was saying' walking slowly, his eyes taking in the scene around him, he carried on talking 'I reckon that they'll take about, two or three weeks, as long as they don't hit any snags. At the same time, the heavy plant will be moving in, so that the foundations for the walls can be dug out, and the cement can be poured'

'How will you secure the site'?

'Most of the stuff, will be kept in the central court yard. The big doors at the front, although they're well knackered, should be strong enough to keep out any intruders'

'Good' after a couple of paces, he turned 'What happens
next'? Monty wasn't just showing interest, he was
extremely excited by what he was having done, and
wanted to get involved, wherever he could.

'Well, in simple terms. Once the wrecking crew have
left, we can put the floor joists in and lay the floors.
Then, the windows can go in, which should mean that the
living quarters are sealed against the weather' looking
out across the river, he watched as a cruise ship sailed
past 'Once the first fix has been done' : -

'First fix'?

'Yeah' when he saw the confused look on Monty's face,
he explained 'The conduit and socket boxes, and so on'

'Oh right' Monty was well out of his depth and he knew
it.

'The plasterers can then do their job. Once that's done,
the sparks can get on with the wiring'

'Sparks'?

'Electricians'

'Oh, I see' he wasn't sure that he did.

'While the sparks are doing their job, the plumbers can
move in, and with a bit of luck, the living quarters will
be up and running inside two months'

'Fantastic'

'You can then move in' Monty grinned, and Duke said
'If you can put up with the noise'

'I'll give it a try and if it gets too much, I'll just move
back to my old house'

'Sounds fair enough to me'

'One thing I'd like too ask, is' even though he was the
one paying the bills, Monty felt strange about asking
questions of the man in front of him 'What are the

chances of getting my office up and running, as soon as poss'?

'I've been thinking about that' Duke had already decided to get his employers office, finished first 'I reckon, that we can get your office at least tidy enough, so that you can work in it, within a week, or two, at the most'

'GREAT'! Monty couldn't keep his enthusiasm out of his voice.

'It will only have temporary electrics and no carpets, but at least you'll be able to work and at the same time' he smiled 'Keep an eye on us'

'Double wammy' Monty joked. After a minute or two of silence, in which both men were lost in their own thoughts, he asked 'Do you know much about the contractors, who will be working here'?

'I have worked with most of them, on and off, for about fifteen years or so' Monty nodded 'Those I know, are all good people' shrugging, he added 'And those that I don't, have all come highly recommended'

'So, no problems expected then'?

'No' Duke shook his head.

'Good' Monty looked at his watch 'Time I wasn't here' he held out his hand 'I'll see you tomorrow'?

'You sure will'

Both men went their separate ways.

Chapter Three

Monty arrived on site by six thirty, the next morning and stood with Duke. Both men were looking up the road, as they waited for the heavy plant to arrive. 'Everything ok Duke'? asked a sleepy Monty.

'Yep. I had a phone call, about forty minutes ago and the plant is well on its way' he looked at his watch 'Should be here at any time' : -

Monty pointed north, towards the horizon 'I think that's them'

'Uh huh. Bang on schedule'

Two hours later, the low loaders had discharged their cargo, and a crane had put in place the temporary site huts, that would be Duke's office and a place for the workmen to eat their meals, for the duration of the project.

First to arrive, were the wrecking crew and the roofers. Duke assigned them their jobs and then walked with them to the place where they were to carry out the work, allotted to them. After running through what was needed and making sure that everybody knew what they were doing, he left them to it. Monty just tagged along, like a waif, bewildered by what was going on.

'Mr. Barrington-Wright' Duke started to ask a question.

'Please, call me Monty' he had already asked Duke to call him by his first name, but it would appear that he had a bit of a problem, with being so familiar.

'Yes, of course, sorry' after giving a little cough, he

carried on 'Monty, will you be here every day, and if so, will you be walking around the site'?
'I'm not sure. Why, will it be a problem'?
'No, not at all. I'm just concerned with health and safety, that's all'
'Oh, right, of course'
'It's just that, if you intend to be here on a regular basis, I may not be able to walk around the site with you every time, and I *will,* have to show you the areas that you can, and can't, go into' this was one thing that he really didn't have time for.
'I understand' he truly did 'In that case, how about, if I only pop in to have a look, let's say twice a week'?
'Sounds good to me, at least that way, I can accompany you and make sure that you don't get into any trouble'
Both men laughed and with that, Monty left. No point in hanging around, there was nothing for him to see and his time could be put to better use elsewhere.

Neither man saw the figure watching them, from the river bank. But had they looked, and had they been able to see the expression on the figures face, then no doubt, they would have been alarmed to see the fear that was so deeply etched into the leathery old skin.

Chapter Four

Over the next few weeks, things moved forward at a satisfying pace. Most of the foundations for the exterior walls, had been laid, the pond had been excavated and the soil, used to landscape the grounds. To say that the pond was big, was an understatement, it should have been called a lake.

Every day that the work was going on, the workmen were watched by a shadowy figure, who stood on the river bank nearby. The person blended in with the surroundings, so well, that they were almost impossible to see. If one of the workers had looked up from their labours, and had they been able to see past the shadows, hiding the watchers face, then they would have looked upon a visage, so grizzled by age and weather, so contorted by fear, or perhaps terror, would be more appropriate, that they could not have been blamed for thinking, that the watcher wasn't human after all, but something from a dark scary place.

Morning turned slowly into midday, then plodded on towards three o'clock, nobody took any notice of the time, all of them too intent on what they were doing, too worry about how long it was before the time came to knock off. Tommy Bryant was making a small, but necessary, alteration to one of the ponds, that he had been excavating from the clay soil, in an area that was to be a completely private part of the gardens. Looking around him, he felt almost as though he were in a crater on the moon. Smiling to himself, he put his spade on the

dark earth and gave it a shove, with his foot. After only
and inch or two, it stopped. Trying again, he sighed when
it wouldn't move.

'Shit' he groaned 'Not more rubble' moving the spade
around, he tried in several different places, before the
blade of the tool finally sank into deep earth 'At least this
bit, isn't as big as some' Tommy mumbled to himself.
With a heave, he prised the clod of soil from the ground.
Something grey caught his attention. This wasn't the
colour of the other detritus, that he had so far dug up. His
curiosity got the better of him, so he lowered himself to
the ground. Kneeling down, he gently started to peel
away the clay, encasing the object, it had been hiding, for
so many years. At first, just little bits came away. Then,
without warning, one large clod broke away, into his
hand. Staring straight into the eyeless sockets, it took
several seconds for his brain to register just exactly what,
he was looking at, but when in did, Bryant stood bolt
upright. His eyes never leaving the sightless skull in front
of him. All of a sudden, the urge to run became too great,
and in a blind panic, he ran straight at the highest part of
the excavation, trying in vain, to climb up the earth wall.
After the third or fourth attempt, to scale the wall, had
failed, he turned around and ran in the opposite direction.
Springing over the lip at the shallow end of the pond, as
if he had been fired from a massive elastic band.

Running as fast as his legs would carry him, he
didn't even see the man in front of him, he just barged
straight through him.

'Tommy'? Bruno said, holding out a mug of tea 'I
thought you might fancy a brew' the other man just hit
his arm at full force, knocking the offered mug, clean out
of his hand. Bruno stood watching his friend, mouth

hanging open, as his eyes fixed on Tommy's receding back. In a flash, he realised that something was wrong. Dropping his own mug, he ran after Tommy.

Duke sat in his office, checking off invoices, when Tommy came thundering through the door, not stopping until he hit the wall opposite, bounced off and ended up in a heap on the floor.

Standing up, Duke looked at the figure before him.

'What on earth has gotten into you Tommy'? when the man just sat staring out through the door, the site manager walked round his desk, crouching down in front of the shaken man. Concern started to climb its way through his veins, when he saw the ashen colour of the labourers face 'Tommy, what is it'? his voice was quiet and encouraging.

Tommy just looked at him for a second, before he swallowed and then stood up. Clearing his throat nervously, he said 'I, I, I've found something that I think you should see'! without waiting for Duke's reply, he climbed to his feet, leading the way back to the pond excavation.

Standing on the edge, looking down, Tommy watched as Duke walked slowly to the heap of dirt, on which the skull rested. Duke asked Tommy to come and join him, but he steadfastly refused.

Chapter Five

Detective Sergeant Hector Farraday stood looking at the heap of soil, on which the skull had been unserermonisoulsy deposited.

'I take it that, that' he pointed at the bony dome 'Came out of there'? he nodded at the hole, at the bottom of the excavation, that he and Duke stood in. Duke nodded

'And how far down are we'?

'About eight, maybe nine, feet, at this point'

'I see' looking around him, he asked 'And what is this going to be'?

'A pond'

'It's a bloody big pond'

'Yeah' Duke nodded 'It's just one of three, that interlink'

D. S. Farraday smiled, as if he understood exactly what was going on 'Can I talk to the guy that found the remains'?

'You can, he's up at the site office, with the owner'

'Ok' he looked at Duke 'Why don't you lead the way'?

At the hut, that served as the site office, Duke introduced the two men, siting quietly talking.

'This is Detective Sergeant Farraday' the policeman nodded amicably 'Mr. Barrington-Wright, the owner, and Tommy' they all shook hands 'Tommy is the one who found the err, remains'

'Do you mind if I have a word with Tommy first'? his question was aimed at Monty.

'No of course not' Monty stood up 'Would you like me

12

to leave'?

'No need for that' he smiled at Monty, before turning his attention back to the other man 'So'! he waited for a second 'You were the poor sod who dug up the skull'? Tommy nodded nervously 'Am I in trouble'? blinking his eyes rapidly, as he looked at the policeman.

'Not unless you're the one who put him in there' when he saw the other man swallow, he asked mischievously You're not, are you'?

'N, n, n, no' Tommy's eyes were wide with panic.

'Good' giving the man his best smile, he carried on 'Did you notice anything unusual, when you were digging in the soil'?

'Like what'?

'I don't know, just anything that looked out of place'? Tommy just shook his head 'Ok Tommy, that's it for now'

'Can I go'?

Farraday nodded 'I may want to talk to you later' he spoke to Tommy's rapidly departing back. looking at Duke he asked 'I take it that your lot, have been told not to go near the crime scene'?

'Of course'?

'Good'!

'You think that whom ever's remains those are, was murdered, then'? Monty asked.

'Until we find out otherwise, then yes, that's how I intend to deal with it' Monty nodded 'Have you lived in the area, a long time'?

'Hm' thinking about his answer, he made a mental calculation 'About twenty' he hesitated for a moment 'Three years, ish' nodding, he added 'Yes. About twenty three years'

'And I take it, you have no ideas about who the remains could be'? Monty shook his head 'And you've never heard any rumours'?

'Not that I can remember, no'

'What about you'? he looked at Duke.

'I don't live around here, so I can't help you there, I'm afraid'

'Hmm' was all Farraday said.

'What happens now'? Duke was concerned about his schedule.

'Scene of Crime and Forensics, will need to have a look, and then, once the crime scene, is finished with, depending on what they find, you can get back to work'

'Any idea how long that will take'?

Farraday shrugged 'From a few days, to a few months' Duke sighed 'I see'

'Don't worry, I'll keep you informed about what's going on'

'Thank you' Duke answered, his voice carrying a grumble.

'So Mr. Barrington-Wright, how much is this little project costing you. If you don't mind me asking'?

'Not at all' doing a quick bit of calculating, he answered 'By the time it's all finished, about three million'

Farraday nodded, before saying 'I'll be in touch gentle men' then he was gone.

Duke and Monty, stood looking at each other.

'Well, this is an unexpected set back' Monty smiled wryly. He had already accepted the fact, that they would probably find something to cause them problems, but this certainly hadn't figured in his plans.

'How long do you think the persons been dead'? asked a frowning Duke.

'Hard to say really, but it could, I suppose, be decades.
Maybe, even before the second world war'
'Why do you say that'?
'I had a look at the plans, when I was thinking about
buying this place, and if I remember correctly, in about
nineteen forty four, the banks were strengthened by
dumping tonnes of soil on the original fortifications, and
the height was increased' his brow furrowed as he
thought 'So I would say that it's a good bet, that our
friend out there, was either in the ground prior to that, or,
was put there at about the same time'
'Hmm' Duke was thoughtful.
'Anyway' Monty was eager to change the subject 'How's
my office coming along'?
'Be finished today'
'Fantastic' Monty rubbed his hands together 'Will it be
safe and secure'?
'Oh yes'
'Good. I can at last start moving my things in, so that I
can start work'
'You sure can'
'Right, I'll be off then'! turning back to Duke, he asked
'If anything else happens, or, you hear anything before I
do, please let me know'
'I will, don't worry'

Chapter Six

Monty stood in his office, looking out of the picture window, at the beautiful view that lay before him. From his vantage point on the top of the old fort, he could see the river Thames for miles, in both directions. Pleased with himself and lost in his own little world, he jumped when there was a knock at the door.

'Come in' he called.

The door swung inwards and Detective Sergeant Farraday stepped in 'Hello Mr. Barrington-Wright'

'D. S. Farraday, how are you'?

'Fine thank you'

'Please have a seat'

Farraday sat down 'Nice office'

'Thank you. I must admit, I am rather pleased' sitting down in his high backed leather chair, Monty asked 'So, what can I do for you'?

'I've come to give you an update'

'Oh, I take it by the look on your face, that the news isn't good'

'I'm afraid not'

'I see'?

'It would appear, that the person found in the bottom of your pond, was murdered'!

'Oh' this wasn't the news, he had wanted to hear 'Is it possible to say how'?

'Oh yes' Farraday sighed deeply 'The person, was shot in the back of the head'!

Chapter Seven

The church was dark, just a single candle burning by the main window, at the front of the ancient building.

Kneeling on the steps, that lead up to the cloth covered alter, was a dark figure, who's shoulders were drooping, as if they were supporting a massive burden. The persons hands were clasped in prayer, head tilted back, as their eyes stared at the figure of Christ on the cross, which was hanging from the ceiling, supported on black chains.

'Forgive me father, for I have sinned' tears ran freely down his stubbled cheeks 'I have strayed and I have done terrible things' a sob broke free from his tightening throat 'I ask for your forgiveness and your strength, to do' : - a noise from behind, made the praying figure stop in mid sentence.

The last things that registered on his senses, were the feeling that someone was standing behind him and then a strange noise, that was a cross between a phut sound, and a puff. Then everything went black, just a fraction of a second, before the praying figure fell forward, to lay in an ever widening pool of blood.

Chapter Eight

'So, who is it'? asked Farraday.

'We have no idea yet, sir' Farraday stood looking at the body, thankful that he was only able to see the back of the victims head, and not the front.

'The woman who does the flowers, she came in to do the arrangements, walked up here and saw' the W. P. C. swallowed 'Him' grimacing, before carrying on 'She thought that perhaps the vicar, had been taken ill. It wasn't until she saw his brains splattered all over the steps, that she realised, it was something worse'

'Nice' Farraday mumbled 'Where is she now'?

'Down stairs, in the, the' she couldn't think of the word she required.

'Vestry' Farraday volunteered.

'Yes sir, the Vestry'

'Ok, I'm going to see if I can have a chat with her' he nodded at the door 'You go and stand guard. Nobody gets in here, without my permission. Is that clear'?

'Yes Sarge'!

Farraday walked quietly down the few steps, that would take him into the Vestry. Gently, he parted the heavy curtain, covering the arched entrance, leading to where the flower lady, who had found the body, sat shakily, drinking a cup of sweet tea. The young constable started to rise, Farraday waved him back to his seat.

'Hallo' the detectives voice, was quiet and calm 'I'm Detective Sergeant, Hector Farraday' the woman just looked at him, with big tear filled eyes 'May I ask your name'? the woman nodded, but said nothing.

'It's Mrs. Hilda Lockhart, Sarge' the constable answered for her.

'Thank you constable' Farraday hid his frustration 'How are you feeling Mrs. Lockhart'? the woman in front of him, didn't move, or utter so much as a groan 'It must have been a bit of a shock for you'?

'Yes' her voice was just a frail whisper.

'Do you feel up to answering a few questions'? he sat in the chair next to her.

'Am I in some sort of trouble'? there was a tremor in her voice.

'No! Certainly not'!

'Only I don't now what I'd do, if I had to go to prison' there was genuine terror in her eyes.

'Mrs. Lockhart. Hilda. Please believe me when I say, you are not in trouble' he patted her hand 'I just need to ask you some simple questions, so that I can get a better picture, of what might, or might not have happened'

'Oh'

'Are you sure you feel able, to answer my questions, only if not, we can do this in a day or two'?

'No' her voice had become a little stronger 'I'll be fine'

'Ok, but if at any time you've had enough, just let me know. Will you do that for me'?

Hilda nodded 'Yes'

'Why don't you start, by telling me what time you got here this morning'?

'About seven thirty' even though she was still obviously nervous, Hilda was starting to calm down a little.

'Is that you're normal time'?

'No, not really' she frowned 'I normally get here around nine o'clock'

'Is there any reason, that you changed your time'?

19

Shaking her head in dismay, she said quietly 'I couldn't sleep, so I got up and decided to come in early' she put a paper tissue, to her eyes 'It's so peaceful here' then, almost as an after thought, added 'It was, before' she didn't finish. It was, however, plain to the two officers, what she meant.

'Ok. Just a few more questions' Farraday glanced at Hilda, just to make sure that she was well enough to go on 'Did you see any body hanging around, when you got here'? Hilda shook her head 'And was the door locked, or unlocked'?

'Locked' she had to think for a moment, as she wasn't a hundred percent sure. Having done the same thing for so many years, that it was now an unconscious part of her routine 'Yes, it was locked'

'Does anybody else, have keys to the church, that you know of'?

'The vicar of course, and one of the church elders, has a spare set. That's it, as far as I'm aware'

'Thank you' Farraday thought for a while, before quietly asking 'Did you recognise the man'?

'What. You mean'? Hilda pointed a finger upwards. 'Yes'

'No' then she added 'Maybe' then she changed her mind 'No'

'Why did you hesitate'? the woman shrugged 'If there's a chance that you recognised the victim, I need to know'?

'I don't want to waste your time' her eyes held the fearfulness again, that had only just gone.

'Why don't you tell me what you know. Then I can decide if I need to investigate it further'?

Hilda smiled at the Detective, she liked him, because he was kind and made her feel at ease 'I thought that he was

20

familiar, but then I thought that I must be wrong'
Farraday didn't interrupt, he just let the woman's thought processes, do their thing 'At first, I thought that it must be the old vicar, but why would he come back after all these years'? the question was asked only half heartedly.
'Do you remember the mans name'?
'What'? Hilda was dragged out of her revere.
'Do you remember the old vicars name'?
Hilda nodded her head 'Oh yes' her face softened 'Morgan Whitacre'
'And what happened to him'?
She looked at him, her face hardening 'Nothing'! she clasped her hands in her lap, saying no more.
'Hilda'? Farraday asked 'What aren't you telling me'? he looked under his eyebrows at her.
'NOTHING'! her chin jutted out defiantly.
Farraday glanced quickly at the P. C. 'Hilda'? his voice held an encouraging tone.
'They were just rumours' when the Detective said nothing, Hilda added huffily 'Unfounded, nasty rumours'
'Why don't you tell me, what those nasty rumours were about'?
'As I said. They were totally unfounded'!
'Ok, but tell me anyway'
After a long defiant look at the young Detective, Hilda spoke quietly, as if to utter the words, that she was about to speak, should never be spoken in church 'They said that he'd' she flushed with embarrassment 'They said that he, he, was having an inappropriate relationship, with a girl young enough to be his daughter'
'And you don't think that these rumours were true'?
'Of course not, my' Hilda stopped herself 'The reverend was a good man. He would never have done anything

21

wrong'

'I take it that he left quickly'?

'Yes'

'Did anything happen, just before he disapeared'?

'I told you, that the rumours weren't true'! she almost shouted at him.

'Hilda' Farraday calmed her 'Sometimes when people leave in a hurry, and people don't know the full details, they have a tendency to fill in the gaps themselves' he smiled 'And as you know, that's how rumours can start' Hilda had started to calm down 'I'm not interested in runours' he lied 'I want facts' he gave what he had just said, a second or two, too sink in 'So Hilda, do you remember if anything happened before, or after, the vicar left'?

'Hmm' the old woman thought, for a moment 'There was this one strange thing'

Chapter Nine

'So, what was this strange thing, that happened'?
'It was so long ago, that I can't really remember'
Farrady was becoming a little frustrated, at the time it
was taking to draw the information out of the elderly
witness.
'All I can remember, is that there was a woman who used
to live out near Bakers Farm' her brow furrowed, as she
tried to think back across the decades 'She lived alone,
as I recall' she nodded to herself 'Yes, that's right.
Anyway, one day she just disappeared. I remember at the
time, there were reports of shooting, but they, the
rumours, to my knowledge, were never confirmed'
'Do you know why she would have been shot'? his
interest had been woken, by what Hilda had just said.
'I don't think that it was the woman, that was shot. As I
said, it was just a rumour'
'So you said. But let's just suppose she was. Do you
know of any reason why, someone would want to hurt
her'? the Detective's eyes shone with eagerness.
'She was a foreigner, but that's not a crime is it'? she
smiled at the Detective.
'No, it's not' taking a deep breath, he asked 'Do you
know where she came from. Originally, I mean'?
'Germany' her answer came instantly, and without pause.
'You seem very sure. Can I ask why'?
'Well. There was the accent of course, but it was
something that she said to my husband, about the war'
her eyes took on a far away look.

'What did she say'?

'Hmm'? Hilda's voice was soft, as if it were coming from a long way off.

'What did this woman say, to your husband'?

'I don't know, but it upset him deeply' she shook her head, as she remembered 'All he would say, was that she dishonoured our boys memory'

Farraday sat thinking,about what he had just been told 'Can I speak to your husband'? Hilda shook her head

'Why'? his question was asked in a quiet, gentle, voice.

'He died three years ago'

'I'm sorry'

The elderly woman, gave him a sad smile 'He's buried out there' Farraday took it, that she meant the graveyard 'That's why I spend so much time here, to be with him, and because I've always done the flowers' quietly, she added 'I took over from my mother'

Farraday smiled 'You've been very helpful Hilda, thank you' standing up, he added 'I'll have a car take you home'

'There really is no need'

'Do you live close by'?

'No, it's about a twenty minute walk'

'In that case, I insist that we give you a lift. You've had a big shock, and I want to make sure that you're ok'

'Thank you'

'Oh, just two more things' when Hilda looked up at him, he carried on 'Would you give your address to the P. C. here'? the woman nodded 'And can I have your husbands first name'?

'Why'? there was suspicion in her look.

'Just for my report, keep everything nice and tidy. That's all'

'Gregory' her voice held an edge.
'Thank you'

     Walking up the stairs, Farraday made his way towards the front of the church. The murder scene, had now been taped off and the area inside the cordon, was a hive of activity. Farraday stood quietly, watching. After about five minutes, a tall man in a paper suite, detached himself from the group of forensic specialists, and walked towards the Policeman.

'Hallo. Are you the officer in charge'?

'Yes, D. S. Farraday'

'Right. I'm David Hickson, the Coroner'

'Good to meet you' the Detective smiled.

'Like wise' Hickson pulled off his rubber gloves and held out his right hand.

After shaking the Coroners hand, Farraday asked 'Can you tell me anything yet'?

'Well, all I can do at this time, is confirm what I suspect you already know'

Farraday invited him to go on 'Please go ahead'

'The victim, is a white male, probably in his early to mid eighties' looking over his shoulder, he glanced back at the scene 'He was kneeling at the time of death, and was killed by a single shot, that went into the back of his head, exciting out through his mouth. Taking most of the bottom jaw with it'

'I take it, that death was instant'?

'Oh yes'

'Do you think the fact, that he was shot here, before the alter, was, or is, significant'

Hickson shrugged 'Who knows. But there are two ways of looking at this murder, I suppose'

'Go on'

'The fact that he was kneeling, could be just a coincidence, him being in a church, it could be that he was simply praying, and was in a convenient position when he was shot. Or' : -

Farraday interrupted 'This was an execution'!

'Exactly'!

'But why would someone want to execute an old man'?

'That dear boy, is for you to find out' the Coroner, turned to go back to work.

'Just one more thing'

'Yes'?

'Is there any forensic evidence, that might link the body in the fort grounds, with this murder'?

'I should be able to answer that, in a day or so'

'Thank you' Farraday had a sneaky suspicion, that there was something nasty brewing, and he didn't like the taste it left in his mouth.

Chapter Ten

Hilda Lockhart turned over in her sleep. After a moment, her eyes slowly opened. Squinting at her bedside clock, she sighed when she realised that it was only just about three thirty, in the morning. Past experience had taught her, that once she was awake, there was no point in trying to go back to sleep. So she got out of bed and slipped her feet into the waiting slippers.

Taking her cocoa to the table, by the dinning room window, she sat looking out into the dark of the early morning. Since her Greg had died, Hilda had trouble sleeping, and so, for the past few years, she had gone through the same ritual, on a nearly daily basis. The next thing that she would do, was the housework, not that it was necessary, as every surface and every ornament, gleamed with polished brilliance. Moving her elbow, absentmindedly, she knocked the writing pad, and pen, that had been resting on its half finished page, onto the floor. Bending down to pick up the errant items, Hilda stopped half way, when she heard a low crack, followed closely by the tinkling of glass. Somewhere deep inside, a warning sound warbled, but still bending forward, she moved quickly off of her chair, straightened up and stepped backwards, deeper into the room. Stopping, she looked around the room. Finally, after she could see nothing out of place, she laughed at herself, muttering under her breath, something about being a stupid old woman. It was at this point, that she noticed the small round hole in the pane of glass, opposite where she had been sitting. Slowly, the realisation that, had she not bent forward to pick up the fallen writing pad, the object that had made the hole, would have hit her in the face. The shock of this revelation, made her slow to react and as she turned to run, in the vain hope of finding somewhere safe to hide, the second, heavy grain bullet, smacked into the side of her neck, exploding out the other side, in a shower of blood and bits of flesh. Knocked sideways and of balance, she tumbled to the floor. Hilda had never been one to give up without a fight, and with surprising strength, for such an outwardly frail woman, she fought the overwhelming tide of unconsciousness, threatening to wash over he, and with clawed fingers, dragged herself towards the door, which lead out into the hallway. Eventually, if only she could stay conscious, her efforts would take her to the telephone near the front door. Somewhere, in the back of her mind, Hilda recognised the sound of the back door being broken in. However, so hard was she concentrating on the mammoth task lying before her, that the implications for her safety, caused by the intruder, never dawned on the small portion of her brain, that was still able to register conscious thought. The very last thing the old woman saw, was a pair of booted feet, placed just in focus of her myopic vision. With a sigh, she finally gave up. What was the point of fighting the inevitable, and besides, this way at least, she got to be with her beloved Greg, earlier than she had anticipated.

P. C. Bradshaw stood looking at the front of the council house. He and his partner, W. P. C. Williams, had been asked to respond to a call, from a worried

28

neighbour, who hadn't seen the elderly woman, who lived here.

Bending down, so that his mouth was level with the letterbox, the P. C. lifted the scarred flap, so that he could shout into the house 'Hello Mrs. Lockhart'? no answer 'Hilda. This is the Police'! still no answer 'Are you ok, only your neighbours are worried'? glancing at W. P. C. Williams, he asked 'Did you try the back gate'? 'Locked' she replied.

Grimacing, Bradshaw bent down to the letterbox again 'Mrs. Lockhart, my name's P. C. Bradshaw and I'm going to break the glass in your front door, so that I can get in, so please don't be alarmed'? standing back, he detached his baton from the belt around his waist.

'Did you manage to get a look, in through the window'? Bradshaw shook his head 'No, the heavy curtains are closed'

Raising his baton, butt end first, the Policeman hit the glass pane, nearest to the lock. Even though he had used minimal force, the glass panel exploded inwards, the wicked looking shards landing on the dark green carpet, some of them standing up, edge on. Knocking out the last remnants of the small window, the P. C. reached through and after a second or two, found the lock release.

Pushing the door open, he stood looking up the hall way. 'Hallo Mrs.Lockhart, are you ok'? nodding at the viscous shards, he said unnecessarily 'Mind the glass' W. P. C. Williams just pulled a face at the man in front of her. When he turned to make sure that she was sticking close to him, she gave him her best smile 'You stick with me, and keep your eyes and ears open'

'You expecting trouble'? even though she wasn't afraid, W. P. C. Niomi Williams, was apprehensive and her eyes kept darting up the stairs, and into the darkness at the top.

'Nah' Bradshaw smiled to himself, as he heard the tremor in his colleagues voice 'She's probably just gone away for a few days, and forgotten to tell anybody' Stopping at the door to the front room, he took his torch from his pocket and after flicking it on, gave the door a gentle push. Nothing happened, he placed his hand on the lever, style handle, pushing it down. With a click, the old fashioned fortress style door, swung open. The beam of Bradshaw's torch burned brightly through the semi-darkness, revealing a scene of total devastation. The front room looked as if a whorl wind had suddenly appeared from nowhere, done its worst and then disappeared. Now the Policeman was really worried. 'Mrs. Lockhart'? he called, but no answer came 'Let's check the back room first. Then we'll do up stairs' 'Right' answered a tense W. P. C. Williams.

Leading the way, Bradshaw trod gently along the hall carpet. Placing a hand on the door, that would open into the dinning room. He glanced over his shoulder at the Police woman and nodded, she answered his unspoken question, with a nod of her own. Listening for any sound that might warn them of an intruder, hiding in wait, the P. C. finally satisfied that, at least for the moment, they were safe, pushed against the surface of the door. The first thing that he saw, as the door swung inwards, was a hand, which obviously belonged to an elderly woman. Slowly, more and more was revealed, until Bradshaw saw the woman's head, laying in a puddle of congealing blood. There was a gasp from behind him, when he looked back, he saw how pale Williams had gone. 'Why don't you go and call this in, and get them to send an ambulance'? looking back at the elderly victim, he added 'Not that they're going to be of much use' Willaims didn't say anything, she just turned and almost ran outside. After taking another look around, the P. C. stepped into the room and knelt down at Hilda Lockharts side. Taking her left wrist in his hand, he checked to see it there was a pulse. Shaking his head, he gently placed her arm back on the floor.

'I've put the call in' looking at Hilda, she asked 'Is she'? Williams couldn't finish her question.

'Dead'? Bradshaw nodded 'I'm afraid so'

'Oh'! she wasn't really surprised.

'We'd better check upstairs and then wait for D. S. Farraday'

D. S. Farraday stood looking down, at the body of Hilda Lockhart.

'Oh Hilda, what is it that you know, that got you murdered'?

'You think that this was deliberate Sarge'?

'Oh yes Winston, that I do'

'But why Sarge. Who would want to hurt an old lady'?

'That, old son, is a very good question'.

Chapter Eleven

'So D. S. Farraday'? said Detective Chief Inspector Hornby 'What's occuring'?

'Looks like we've got ourselves another murder'!

'Really'?

'I'm afraid so' Farraday looked out across the back lawn. From his vantage point by the kitchen window, he could see to the bottom of the garden.

'Have forensics finished here'?

'Yes'

'In that case, you can put the kettle on'

'Sir, I don't think that that would be appropriate'

'Hector' Hornby said, with mock patience 'The poor old girl in there' he pointed over his shoulder, with the thumb of his right hand 'Isn't going to mind, is she'? when Farraday said nothing, he repeated his request 'So, put the kettle on'!

'Sir'

'Have you found out anything yet'?

'No' Farraday clicked the kettle on 'We've had a neighbour in, to see if she could tell us if anything is missing, but we drew a blank there. It would appear that nothing has been taken. Nothing obvious, anyway'

'So, what is you're take on the situation'? Hornby frowned, as he waited for an answer, his eyes roaming around the interior of the kitchen.

'Looks like someone was either trying to find something, and Hilda disturbed them, paying the price. Or, she was murdered to keep her quiet'

'Quiet about what'?

'I think that she ties in, with the body found in the grounds of the fort, and also the body in the church'

'Why on earth, would you think that they're all linked'?

Hornby shook his head in frustration, for a normally intuitive and intelligent man, the D. S. could be very dense, sometimes.

'The village of Old Acres, is hardly a hot bed of crime, so when a body turns up, followed by another two, withins days of each other, you can bet your life savings, that there is a link joining them all'

'What is this mythical link, then'?

'I have no idea, but I'm damn sure going to find out'

'Ok Hector, I want you to keep me informed, and I warn you' he gave the junior Detective, a hard stare 'If this gets out of hand, like the incident in Broadoak, then you'll be the one to cop the flak'

'Why doesn't that surprise me'? Farraday mumbled sarcastically, under his breath.

'What'? snapped Hornby.

'Nothing sir. I was just thinking out loud' Farraday smiled at his superior.

'Make sure this is wrapped up quickly'! without so much as a good bye, Hornby turned and left the crime scene.

Chapter Twelve

Detective Sergeant Hector Farraday, sat at his desk, reading the preliminary reports, emailed to him by David Hickson, the Coroner. As he perused them, a thought struck him. Picking up his phone, he dialled the extension of Bridget Mullins, the station girl Friday.

'Bridget, will you come in for a moment please'? without a word the woman put the phone down.

'Yes Hector' her manor was brusque, not something you would normally associate with her.

'You ok Bridget, only you seem a bit' : - he was cut off in mid sentence.

'I'm fine'! her eyes told another story.

Farraday shrugged, it really wasn't his problem 'Would you do a search please, on these names' he placed a piece of paper on the desk, in front of him and started writing, listing the names that he wanted the information on, his script was small and spidery. When he'd finished, he handed the sheet of paper to the woman, in front of him. After squinting at the hand writing for several seconds, she read out the names 'Morgan Whitaker. Hilda Lockheart. Gregory Lockheart' frowning, she looked at the Policeman 'Is that it'?

'Yes' the D. S. was becoming tired of the secretaries persistent grouchiness.

'What, no background information'? Bridget's jaw, was set in an argumentative line.

'Bridget'?

'Yes'?

'Just bloody do it'!

Without a word, she turned and on her way out, slammed the door so hard that the filings in Farraday's teeth rattled. Shaking his head, Farraday went back to reading the Coroners report.

Victim number: 1.

Male: Aged between late teens and early 30's.

Height: 5ft. 11ins.

Weight: Unable to determine accurately. But, we can estimate his weight, by the remains of his clothes. That estimate would put him at about 154 pounds.

Hair: Dark brown.

Estimated time of murder: Taking into consideration, the style of clothes, shoes and watch. I would suggest, around the mid 1940's.

Cause of death: A single gun shot to the rear of the head.

Other significant indicators: Due to the broken bones in his hands, feet and broken ribs, I would suggest, that the victim was tortured and then murdered.

This is as much as I can determine at this time.

Victim number: 2.

Male: Aged between late 70's and late 80's.

Physical condition: This man was physically fit, for his age. There is some wearing of joints, and an indication that the victim suffered from mild arthritis. As you would expect in a man of this age. However, this man has obviously led a healthy life, this is evident, by the condition of his vital organs.

Cause of death: A single gun shot, to the rear of the head.

Distinguishing marks: Blemish on the left thigh, just off the mid line and towards the top of the leg. Scar on left cheek, just under the bottom eye lid. There are also a series of numbers tattooed on the inside of the left wrist. I would suggest, that this is possibly a registration mark, from a Concentration camp.

Victim number: 3.
Female: Mrs. Hilda Lockhart.
Aged: 79.
Physical condition: Enlarged heart and early signs of lung cancer. There are also, signs of cirrhosis of the liver. There is no other evidence of any physical illness.
Cause of death: A single gunshot to the neck. Causing massive tissue damage and loss of blood.
Estimated time of death: Within the last forty eight hours.

Farraday put down the Coroners report and lent back in his chair.
'So'? he said, to the crack in ceiling 'The victims seem to be from the same age group. Within a few years, at any rate. The bones that were found in the fort grounds, look like they could be from a man, also of the same age group' one more thing struck him. If the murder victim from the church was imprisoned in a Concentration camp, could it be assumed, that he was Jewish? And, if Hilda Lockhart, was, correct, in believing him to be the vicar, of the local church, why was a person from the Jewish faith, preaching in a church, belonging to a Gentile religion? All interesting questions, that only served to act as a millstone around his neck. What he needed to do, was have a look around Hilda's house, on his own.

Pulling up outside number 2 Pond Lane, Farraday
sat looking at the house.
'What secrets are you hidding'? he asked the two story
dwelling.
Taking a torch from the side pocket of his car, he then
patted his jacket pocket, to make sure that he had the
keys, to Hilda's house.
Standing in the hallway, Farraday stood listening
to the silence.
'Come on' he said quietly 'Talk to me'
Walking into the front room, he stood in the centre of the
floor. Looking around, he shook his head. Judging by the
state of the room, every draw had been taken out and
emptied onto the floor. The sofa and the two armchairs,
had been ripped to pieces. All the pictures had been
broken and the carpet had been pulled off of the grips.
The scene had been repeated all over the house.
'This house has been cleansed' Farraday spoke to
himself, unaware that he was not alone.
'Talking to yourself Sarge'?
Farraday spun round 'STEVE'! he held out his hand,
which was taken eagerly 'What are you doing back so
early'?
'I heard that you were having a bit of trouble, so I
guessed that you would need some expert help' Steve
Lucas grinned.
'Yeah right' Farraday smiled to himself 'Why don't we
go and sit in the kitchen, so that I can bring you up to
speed'?

Chapter Thirteen

'So'? Farraday said 'There you have it. Two murders and one probable murder. We have found no links yet, but Bridget, is searching for any background on the names we have'

'I'm curious about one thing' Lucas frowned.

'What's that then'?

'Well, if the man found in the church was Jewish, why was he a Church of England Vicar'?

'That's what we need to find out'

'Could he have been using his job, as some sort of cover'?

'But what could he possibly have to cover up'?

'I have no idea. But perhaps he had a past that he didn't want anybody to know about'

'Or, perhaps the tattoo, on his arm, is meant to deceive us'

Lucas nodded 'I take it that you're here, looking for inspiration'? looking around the room, his nose wrinkled, as he took in the out of date decor.

'Yep' was all Farraday said.

'But you haven't received any yet, I take it'?

'Nope'

Lucas stayed where he was 'Did the forensics team, turn up anything'? the Detective shook his head 'But you think that they missed something'?

'It's unlikely, but'? something nagged at him 'I think that what they may have missed, isn't necessarily a physical piece of evidence, as such, but is part of, or the cause of, her murder'

'Which you think, links the other two'?

'Yes'

'Why don't we look at this, from another perspective'?

'Like what'?

'I don't know' then Lucas smiled, and in a vastly over done, American hero's voice, said 'Look at everything. See everything. Rule out nothing. Even the most ridiculous of ideas! Look at the crime scene through the eyes of a criminal. And' : -

Farraday interrupted him 'Ok. ok, I get the idea' shaking his head, he added 'Very ham. But I get your point'

Lucas smiled 'Why don't you start down here, and I'll go upstairs'?

'Ok' Lucas had started looking, before his senior was out the door. When he found nothing, he moved into the front room.

  The door into the lounge, was open and Lucas stood on the threshold looking in. Nothing had been moved or tidied up. The room still looked as if a bomb had gone off, causing a vacuum that had sucked everything onto the floor. Placing his feet carefully, he made his way into the room, watching where he was going, as he went. Stopping, he used the toe of his shoe to flip over a photograph. Taking a pair of latex gloves from his jacket pocket, carefully pulling them on, Lucas crouched down and picked up the photo. The sepia image showed a newly married couple, the woman in a lace wedding dress, holding a small bouquet and the man, in a well tailored suite. The woman, whom he assumed was Mrs. Lockhart, had had her cheeks painted red and the flowers had been brightened to a slightly dull yellow. The young Detective smiled, his grandparents had some photographs on their mantelpiece, taken in the same era. The photographer had also added the colouring afterwards, when the negative had been developed. Something about the images worried him and he looked around for some more. After he'd gathered about seven or eight, he fanned them out in his left hand, almost as if he were playing cards.

'Find anything'? Farraday asked, as he stood watching Lucas study each photo in turn, very closely.

'Not sure' his answer absentminded, as he concentrated on the images before him. Looking up, he frowned, as he walked over to Farraday 'Take a look at these, Hector' after handing the brown tinged images to his fellow Detective. Giving him a minute to look at them, he asked 'Notice anything strange about them'?

The senior Detective look up at him, then gave each of the photos, one more scrutinising stare 'No' he scowled.

'What period of time, do you think they were taken in'? he kept the smile, that was trying to break out, firmly hidden.

'I'm no expert, but I would say' Farraday thought for a moment 'Perhaps the forties or early fifties'

'Probably during the war then'?

'Yes, possibly' he wasn't quite sure where this was going.

'So why isn't the man wearing a uniform'?

'I don't know. Maybe he didn't want too'?

'But it was customary at the time, or so I believe, to get married in uniform'

'Perhaps he didn't have one'

'Why'?

'Perhaps he was a conscientious objector'?

'Or a spy'? Lucas released the smile, that had been

40

straining to get loose.

Farraday looked heavenwards 'You've been watching too many films'

'Doesn't it strike you as strange, that there are no pictures of the war. You know what your trouble is'? Lucas raised his eyebrows.

'No. But I get the feeling you're going to tell me' Farraday wore a look of frustration.

'You've got no imagination' smiling cheekily, Lucas said 'So, what's next'?

'Hmm'? his brow furrowed, as he thought 'When I interviewed Hilda' Lucas raised his eyebrows, questioningly 'Mrs. Lockhart' Farraday clarified for his friend 'She told me about a woman, that used to live out by Bakers farm. A German woman, who disappeared suddenly'

'What sort of time line are we talking about'?

'Fifty or sixty years ago, maybe'

'Ok' this wasn't going to be easy 'Have you any idea of the address'?

'No. But I got the impression that it was a house on its own'

'Was her disappearance reported at the time'?

'Yes, I believe so, and there were also gun shots reported at the time'

'So why don't we have a look at the report, and then we can get the address'?

'That could take days. I'll have someone check that angle out, but in the mean time, I want you to have a snoop around' Lucas was just about to object, but the senior Detective stopped him 'Steve'? Lucas looked at him 'Just do it'!

'Right' turning away, he grimaced as he went to do as

41

he'd been ordered.

Chapter Fourteen

Driving through the white painted wrought iron gates, at the head of the avenue, that would lead eventually, to the big manor house where the present owner of Bakers Farm, lived, it quickly became clear to D. C. Lucas, just how wealthy this farm owner was. There was something in the way, that the buildings were looked after, coupled with the landscaping, of the massive gardens, that screamed money, and plenty of it. Not that he was jealous, money had never worried him, as long as he had enough to pay the bills, he was happy. Not only that, large amounts of money, brought its own problems. Parking his car, next to a late model Mercedes estate, Lucas got out of his dirty vehicle and took the wide steps to the front door, two at a time. After pressing the brass bell push, twice, Lucas stood and patiently waited. Slowly the front door opened, and a pair of dark eyes peered out at him. Seconds later, a woman's voice spoke to the child owner of those eyes.

'Pauli, what have I told you about opening the front door? Now go and play with your sister'!

The boys face disappeared and the door opened wider, to reveal an attractive woman, in her mid fifties.

'Can I help you'? her voice was friendly and helpful.

'Yes' Lucas took out his warrant card. Holding it up, so that the woman could see it clearly 'I'm Detective Constable Steve Lucas' he lowered the wallet 'I was wondering if I might ask you a few questions'? he smiled hopefully.

'Yes of course' she stood back and let him in 'If you'd like to go in there' she pointed to a room, to the left of the hallway 'We can talk without being interrupted by the children'

After they had both settled into comfortable chairs, in the small study, the Policeman asked 'Do you own the farm'?

'No. Well yes' an embarrassed smile caused fine lines, at the side of her eyes and the corners of her mouth, to deepen 'That is, it's my husband who owns the farm'

'May I take his name'? Lucas had taken a small brightly coloured note book, from an inside pocket.

'Nice' she said jokingly.

'My daughter bought it for me' it was his turn to smile 'And made me promise to use it'

'Children' she said, as if that one word explained everything.

'I was asking about your husbands name'

'Oh yes. Sorry' she looked at his notepad 'Hunt. John Hunt'

'Thank you. And may I ask your name'?

'Of course. Constance'

'Ok'

'So, are we in some sort of trouble'? her eyes darkened slightly, with worry.

'No. It's nothing to do with you' Lucas smiled reassuringly 'I was just wondering, if I could ask your husband, if he knew about a woman that used to live near your farm, some years ago'?

'My husband is away on business, but I'm sure I can help you' she added for good measure 'I was brought up on the farm'

'Oh right' clearing his throat, as quickly as he could, he

then said 'I'm looking for a house, where a woman lived on her own. The woman was probably German, and the house stood on its own' grinning, he added 'I'm afraid, that that's all the information I have'

'That's ok. I think I know exactly where you mean'

'You do'? surprise echoed in his words.

'Yes'

'Is it near here'?

'About twenty minutes walk, or five minutes in the car'

'Would you mind, telling me how to get there by car'?

'I could take you, if you like'?

'That's very kind of you, but I've disrupted your day enough already' that wasn't the true reason, he just wanted to snoop around on his own.

'Ok, but I don't mind really'!

'Thank you, but I think I'd best do this on my own'

'Ok' there was disappointment in her voice 'When you come to the main road, turn right and about a mile further on, you'll come to another turning on the right, it's just an old farm track, but it'll take you where you want to go. Drive to the end and that's the house, I think you're talking about' she shivered, as old childhood memories came back to haunt her.

'Thank you' Lucas stood up.

'I'll show you out'

'There's no need' turning, he started to walk out of the room, then stopping, he looked back 'Thank you' was all he said.

'My pleasure' Constance gave him a warm smile.

Ten minutes later, Lucas brought his car to a stop, at the end of the track. He would have been there sooner, but having missed the entrance, he had to turn around and go back. Standing quietly, the Detective looked at the old house, more of a cottage really, and wondered if anybody actually lived there. Although it wasn't exactly derelict, it would be hard to imagine that it was habitable either.

After glancing at the sign, that had been written in white paint, the letters having run before they had had time to dry, giving a kind of melting effect. Lucas ignored the "PRIVATE PROPERTY" and "DANGER KEEP OUT" warnings. Pushing on the wooden picket gate, which gave in and just simply fell apart, ending up in bits on the path, that lead to the front door. Carefully, the Detective picked his way through the remains that lay before him, and walked to the front of the house. Gingerly, he stepped onto the porch, that guarded the door, from the worst of the weather. Looking at the flaking paint, the colour of which had once made the door stand out against the darkness of the surrounding trees, Lucas chose a spot and knocked, not to hard just in case the old wood crumbled to dust. No answer came. Not that he expected someone to respond, so he tried once more, just for luck. When the only reply he received was silence, he stepped back and looked up at the dirty, grime encrusted windows, that had once let light into, what he assumed, were bedrooms. Turning right, Lucas tried to look into the first window he came to, but what remained of heavy drapes, had been pulled shut, so he moved on. Picking his way with care, through the briars, which had taken over almost the whole back garden, he slowly made his way to the back of the house.

Standing on tip toe, he tried to look into a window, that had been built into the wall, about six feet above the ground. The only thing that he could see, was the same grimy blackness, that seemed to shroud the inside of the house, as if it were jealously guarding a secret from prying eyes. Lucas was just deciding whether to carry on looking around, or to give up, when he heard what sounded like a twig breaking behind him. Slowly, he turned to face a powerfully built man, of about seventy five. The most striking thing about the man, who stood before him, was his eyes. Lucas had never seen such anger, in someones eyes before, and he was in no doubt, that if he didn't tread carefully, he could be in a lot of trouble.

'**CAN'T YOU READ**'! the man was well spoken and very, very, angry.

'Yes. But' : -

'**BUT NOTHING**'! the man took a step forward, his whole body tensed, as if he were getting ready to strike '**THIS IS PRIVATE PROPERTY AND YOU'VE NO RIGHT TO BE HERE**'! his words were clipped and it was obvious, from the way that he spoke, that he was an educated man, although the clothes that he was wearing, tended to cast doubt, on that supposition.

'I'm sorry if I've offended you' Lucas smiled, in the hope that it might calm the stranger down, but the only thing to happed, was the man taking another step forward, his hands clenched into fists 'if you'll just let me explain' : - '**I'M NOT INTERESTED IN YOUR LIES**'! the stranger spat at Lucas's feet.

The Detective jumped back '**HEY**'! he shouted '**There's no need for that**'! his own anger was starting to rise to the surface.

'**ARE YOU GOING TO GET OFF MY LAND, OR AM I GOING TO HAVE TO THROW YOU OFF**'?

'I wouldn't advise that you try'

'OH AND WHY'S THAT. YOU SOME KIND OF MARTIAL ARTS EXPERT'? his voice was full of sarcasm, and there wasn't a trace of fear, almost as if he knew that the Policeman was no match for him.

'No' Lucas smiled 'I'm a Policeman'

The angry stranger, looked at him, then asked in a voice full of suspicion **'What sort of Policeman'**?

'A Detective'

'Military or civilain'? although the stranger was still alert, his anger seemed to have lost its edge.

'Civilian'

The older man took a step back.

'What do you want'? his voice was inquisitive, his question asked in a blunt, rood manner, but his previous anger was, it would appear, starting to cool.

'I was hoping to find out some information, about a woman who used to live here' Lucas watched the other man closely.

'How do I know you're who you say you are'? his old suspicions started to surface.

Lucas went to put his right hand, into his jacket pocket, but when the older man jumped back, he stopped moving and looked at him quizzical 'If it's ok with you, I can show you my I. D'? the stranger gave a curt nod. Taking the leather wallet, that held his warrant card, from his inside pocket, Lucas opened it up and handed it to the other man, who checked it closely. Then, with a grunt, handed it back.

'So, now you know my name, why don't you tell me yours'?

'Why'?

'Because it's better than having to call you, thingy, or, errm'

'Beecher. Eustace Beecher' he gave his name, almost sulkily.

'Well, Mr. Beecher, why don't we start again'? when Beecher just stood staring at him, the Policeman asked 'Do you live here'? he nodded at the old house.

'What's it to you'? asked Beecher belligerently.

'Look. All I want to know, is do you live here. Yes or no'?

'Yes. Well sort of'

'What's that supposed to mean'? Lucas was becoming frustrated, at Beecher's refusal to give him a straight answer.

'It means' Beecher smiled, for the first time 'That sometimes I live here, and sometimes I don't'

'Are you living here now'?

'Yes'

'Good' Lucas returned the other mans smile.

'At least we got that sorted out'

'What is it that you want to know'? his voice had taken on a conciliatory tone.

Looking around, the Detective asked 'Is there somewhere that we can sit down'?

Taking a bunch of keys from his trousers pocket, Beecher chose a Yale key, and opened the back door. Stepping inside, he used his right hand to flick on the light switch.

'Make yourself at home' he pointed to a chair, that had been pushed tidily against a small drop leaf table.

'Thank you' Lucas looked around the kitchen. Surprise took him over, as he realised just how clean and tidy it was.

'Would you like a drink'? without waiting for an answer, he filled a kettle and plugged it in.

'Yes please'

'So, who is it that you want to know about'? before the other man answered, he enquired about the womans' name 'What is the woman's name'?

'I have no idea' great start, he thought.

'Oh well, that narrows the field a bit' taking two mugs down, from a cupboard, over the work top, he asked 'Tea or coffee'?

'What ever's going'

'Coffee it is then'

'The only information that I have, is that she lived on her own, and she was foreign' Lucas saw with interest, that Beecher's back had straightened, almost imperceptibly, but still enough to show that, what he'd heard, had stirred him in some way 'Possibly German'

'I don't know anybody like that, ever having lived here' he turned to face Lucas 'So if you don't mind, I have a lot of things to do'! walking to the back door, he placed his hand on the handle, but turned to look back into the room, when he realised that Lucas hadn't moved

'I said': -

'I heard what you said, and I don't believe you'

'**How dare you**'! Beecher's face, had started to turn crimson.

'Why don't you cut the crap, so that we can get down to the nitty gritty'?

'If you think' : - Beecher was getting ready to launch an all out defence.

'**MISTER BEECHER**'! Lucas voice carried authority '**Please sit down**'!

'**I**' : -

'**I won't tell you again**'!

Beecher reluctantly sat down, opposite the Detective.

'Thank you' leaning back in his chair, he frowned 'Now,

50

why don't you tell me, what you know'?

Chapter Fifteen

'I don't know much' Beecher lied.

'So tell me what you do know' Lucas had lost most, of his earlier patience, and would have been just as happy, to be continuing their conversation down at the Police station.

'I moved into the area, just after the war' his mind wandered back, as his voice became sad 'I'd lost all my family in a bombing raid' snapping back to the present, his voice took on its former strength 'I rented a couple of rooms, in a big house, not far from here' a smile lightened his face, as happy memories started to flood his mind 'I often used to come for a walk this way, and had always liked this cottage' coughing to clear his throat, he looked directly at Lucas 'Imagine my surprise, when I found out that it was owned, by a foreigner. What's more, a German at that' he grinned 'Not that I expect you to understand'

'Oh I think I can understand, how you felt. Even if I don't necessarily agree'

'You youngsters have no idea' : - the anger he felt, wasn't aimed at Lucas, so he stopped and took a deep breath 'Sorry'

'There's no need to appologies'

'Maybe not, but the war has nothing to do with you, and anyway. It's all a long time ago'

'Did you ever talk to the woman'?

'Just the one time' frowning, he changed his mind 'No. Maybe a couple of times'

'Do you remember the content of those conversations'?
'Not the exact words, no'
'That doesn't matter, just give me an idea of what was said'
'Ok' Beecher thought for a moment 'The first time we met, I think that I just said, hallo. But when I found out that she was German, things didn't go to well' he started to fidget 'I didn't speak to her for some time after that. But the next conversation we had, was not a very friendly one' not wanting to go on, he stopped.
'Go on'
'I'm not very proud of what I said'
'Never mind. Just tell me'
'I had a go at her, for having the audacity to come and live in my country. The country, that her and her crew, had tried to destroy'
'What did she say to that'?
'Nothing, not then. But when I asked, how come she had been able to come here, in the first place. And how could she afford to buy this place'? raising his hands, he indicated the cottage 'She said something about "It's not only, what you know. But also, who you know" he paraphrased.
'Did you understand what she meant. Or who she was talking about'?
'Not then, no'
'But you do now'?
'Maybe. Maybe not'
Sighing, Lucas said 'Please, don't go all moody on me again'
'You miss understand me'Lucas raised his eyebrows questioningly 'I'm not "going all moody"' Beecher grinned 'I just mean, that I have a theory, but no hard

facts'

'I see' Lucas sat waiting patiently, but when his host stayed quiet, he verbally prodded him 'Are you going to let me in on your theory'?

'If you're interested'

'I am'!

'Well, given the fact that it was not long after the war, and also, taking into consideration, my suspicion that she was German, although I have no exact proof of this, I suspected that she may have been a spy. On top of that, her comments about "Knowing people", made me believe at the time, and I still do, that she may well have been a double agent'

'Or someone, purely working for us'

'Of course'

'I hear that she disappeared suddenly, is that correct'?

'I'm not sure about *suddenly*, but she did go quickly'

'Same thing, surely'? this question was meant to draw Beecher, out.

'Not at all. Suddenly, could mean, there one night, gone the next. Quickly, could mean, gone in a couple of days'

'So, where do you think she went'?

'I have no idea'

Lucas believed him 'What, no theories'? he joked.

'Only one'! his voice carried a serious note.

'Go on'?

'I think, I heard a shot, or maybe two. But again, I have nothing solid to go on'

'I heard, that there was a rumour, going around at the time'

'It wasn't started by me'

'I don't doubt that for a minute. But you misunderstand me' Lucas frowned 'I am wondering, what those rumours were saying'? looking at Beecher, he waited for him to go on.

'They said that, she had been murdered by the people she worked for'

'And who might "They" be'?

'I have no idea' the look on his face said otherwise.

'That's not exactly true, is it'?

Beecher shrugged 'No. I guess not'

'Why don't you tell me, what it is that you know'?

'Is that an order'? his voice had taken on a churlish tone.

'No' Lucas sighed 'It's a request'

'Are you always, this patient'? Beecher chuckled.

'No'!

'Thought not' sitting back, he studied the younger man, for a moment **'If**, and I do mean **if**, the stories, going around at the time, were true. Then I think, she was either scared off, or she was' shrugging, he grimaced 'Murdered, to shut her up'

'But why would someone, want to shut her up'?

'Because she knew something that made her dangerous'

'But dangerous to who'?

Beecher moved his chair, the movement, stiff and awkward. Suddenly, Lucas got in inkling, of just how old the man in front of him, truly was.

'Given, that we're talking just a few years after the second world war, I suppose we couldn't be blamed for thinking, that it could have something to do with espionage, of some sort'

'But what could she possibly have known, that would put her in danger'?

'We could be talking about anything, and anyone here'

'This is getting me nowhere' Lucas's frustration, was

starting to show.

'What do you expect, an instant answer'? Beecher shook his head 'What ever happened, happened sixty years ago'

'I know, but' : -

'Why the sudden interest'?

'We think that this may have something to do, with a case we're working on' Lucas was reluctant to say more.

'Oh. I take it, you mean, the body found in the grounds of the fort, and the other two murders'?

'How did you know about them'?

'This is a small village, bad news travels quickly' giving Lucas his best smile, he asked 'Is that it then, only I need to get a move on'?

'Just a couple more questions'

Beecher sighed 'Go on then'

'How long have you lived here. In this house, I mean'?

'Why'? it was his turn to be suspicious.

'Just curious'

The Detective had seen the expression, that had momentarily masked Beecher's face, before it had evaporated, into the non-committal vagueness, that he now wore. That look also held something else, something akin to fear.

Shrugging painfully, Beecher mumbled his answer 'Twenty odd years' his eyes were fixed on the table top, as if it held some morbid interest for him.

'Why did you buy this place'?

'**I told you**'! the older mans voice, had started to rise, showing his anger '**I'd liked it for a long time, and when I got the chance, I bought it**'!

'But why'd you take so long to purchase it. After all, you seemed pretty desperate to have it'?

'**NOW LOOK, I'VE**' : - his fear was starting to grow,

and he was hoping that if he could hide it, behind a show of anger, he would be able to fool this young Policeman. 'It's a perfectly reasonable question' Lucas smiled, as he interrupted the mans show of belligerence.
'**AND I TOLD YOU. THAT I'M BUSY**'!
'So answer my questions, and I'll go'!
'**Alright. Alright**'! he wiped his mouth, with the back of his hand. A subconscious move, that was a physical expression of his nervousness 'I tried to buy it soon after the woman disappeared, but whoever owned it, wasn't selling'
'How do you know, they wouldn't sell'?
'Because I left several notes, asking them to contact me, if they were interested in selling. But they never did'
'So how did you come, to finally buy it then'?
'Some years later, it came up for sale, so I bought it through an Estate Agent'
'Who are they'?
'Were they'!
'What do you mean "were"'?
'They went bust'
'I see' how convenient 'What *was,* their name'?
Beecher smiled to himself 'McKlintock's, in the high street'
'Hmm'? Lucas decided, that he had gone as far as he could, with the questioning. For now, anyway, and so, he asked 'Do you mind if I have a look around'?
'Why'? Beecher's voice range with his alarm 'Do you have a search warrant'?
'Do I need one'? Lucas was becoming more suspicious, and therefore, more interested, by the minute.
'N. n. no. Of course not' Beecher looked at his watch 'It's just that I'm late already' he left the rest of the

sentence, unspoken.

'Ok' Lucas stood up 'Thank you for your help' when the older man, went to stand up, he added 'Please don't get up, I can find my own way out'

Beecher stood watching the Detective, through a small slit in the drapes, that covered the front room window. "He's going to be trouble" he thought to himself "And if he becomes a nuisance, he'll have to be silenced". Turning away from the window, he took a mobile phone from the breast pocket, of his shirt, and punched in a series of numbers.

'We've got a possible problem'! was all he said, before hanging up.

Chapter Sixteen

'So'? Farraday said, as he looked up at D. C. Steve Lucas
'Did you find the house'?

'Oh yes, I found it alright'

'And did you learn anything'? Farraday, had picked up
on the note of excitement, in Lucas's voice.

'I did' he smiled 'I believe, that the person who owns the
house, is lying about how much he knows, about our
German woman'

'Really'? perhaps this case wasn't, going to be so hard to
crack, after all.

'Yes, and Mr. Beecher, that's the name of the owner, was
very reluctant, to let me have a look around'

'Is that so'! standing up, the senior Detective smiled at
the D. C. 'Perhaps, we should make another visit to Mr.
Beecher. And this time, we'll have a warrant. Just in
case'! patting Lucas on the back, he praised his work
'Well done Stevie boy, you've done well'

'So, when do we go back'?

'As soon as I can get the paper work done'!

Chapter Seventeen

Marcus Merrik sat looking at the note, that he was holding, in his right hand.

'Oh dear' he said to himself 'This isn't good at all'!

The A4 sheet, that he was reading, was headed.

"NATIONAL SECURITY AGENCY"

Underneath, was a classification code.

"N. S. A. EYES ONLY"

Followed by.

"AMBER WARNING"

Notification of receipt of request, for information on subjects, under: **"RED FLAG PROTECTION"**

"CODE NAMES"

BRIAR = DECEASED.

HOBBO = DECEASED.

ARTHUR = DECEASED.

WING = INACTIVE.

ROBIN = DECEASED.

Origin of request: Essex Police.

Course of action: Yet to be determined.

     Placing the notification, on the desk in front of him, Merrik put his head in his hands.
'What is it that they say about, your pigeons coming home to roost'? looking up he sighed 'We should have put this to bed years ago'! picking up the phone he barked and order, when his secretary answered '**Get me Crabshawe**'!

Chapter Eighteen

D. S. Hector Farraday sat at his desk, flicking through the new reports, that had been sent from Scene of Crimes and the Coroners office. It didn't take long. 'Great'! Farraday grumbled, as he threw the collective folders back onto his desk 'Shouldn't have wasted the people' what both sets of reports confirmed, was that nothing much had changed, from the initial findings. All the victims had died, from a single gun shot wound. The murder victim, who's body had been uncovered at the fort, had died of a head wound, as had the victim at the church. The last person, had bled to death, due to a neck wound. S. O. C. O. found nothing at any of the murder sites, that would help identify the victims, with the exception of Hilda Lockhart. Neither had any of the bullets been found.

There were, however, several things that worried Farraday about this case, and he suspected, obviously, that they were all linked.

A mental image of his hand, came into his mind, as he counted off his concerns, a finger was raised.

Worry number one: Due to the way that two of the victims were murdered, judging that they *were,* murdered, and he doubted, that there was any other explanation, he would guess that they had been executed.

Worry number two: Mrs. Lockhart. Was she executed, or, was she just in the wrong place, at the wrong time.

Even with todays occurrence of violent robberies, it was still unusual for a domestic burglar, to carry a gun, let alone, actually shoot someone. So, it looked as if she had disturbed someone, who was looking for something, and had paid the price. Was she involved? if not, why was her house ransacked?

Worry number three: If Mrs. Lockhart wasn't involved, was it her dead husband that was the problem?

Flicking a button on the intercom, sitting by his telephone, he said 'Bridget'?
'Yes Hector'?
'Will you get me a copy, of the death certificate, for a Mr. Gregory Lockhart. He died about three years ago'
'Yes'
Farraday let go of the button.

Worry number four: How was the German woman involved. If at all? and did the new owner of the cottage, have any connection with the case'?

"At this rate" Farraday thought "I'm gonna run out of fingers"
The door to his office opened, and he was startled from his deep thinking, by the voice of D. C. I. Trevor Hornby.
'Well Hector, how's it going'?
Farraday was disturbed to see that, his superiors face held an almost plastic smile 'I take it, that you're talking about our murder cases'?
'Of course' his voice held a kind of guarded note, to it.
'Slowly' Farraday watched the other man, closely.
'I see'

'We keep finding more loose ends, and so far, we have no way of tying them up'

'So, you're saying, that this case is unsolvable'? there was a gleam of hope, in his eyes.

'No, of course not. It's far to early to tell'! there was something going on here, that was making him very suspicious 'Why do I get the feeling, that I'm going to be told something that I won't like'?

Hornby licked his lips. He wished that this case, had been taken on by one of the other Detectives. One that he could manipulate, for his own ends. Unfortunately, Farraday wasn't one of them, as he had found out, Very soon, after Farraday had joined them. Again he licked his lips. After coughing nervously, he spoke. His voice held an unmistakable note of command.

'I want you to bury this case'!

'Why'? the younger man asked calmly.

'Because I'm telling you to'! the colour was starting to rise, from below his shirt collar.

'NO'! was all Farraday said.

'This isn't a request. It's an ORDER'!

'Then I want to know why'? still, he was remarkably calm.

'I don't have to explain myself, to YOU'! standing up, Hornby glared down at the Detective, who was still sitting behind his desk.

'NO'!

'You do as I order, or I'll have you suspended'!

'Fine, go ahead'! his eyes never left those of his superior 'I'm sure there's a lot of people, who would be interested as to why, I was being suspended for doing my job'!

'Are you threatening me'? his eyes narrowed, in suspicion.

'No sir. I'm just telling you how it is'
'**WHY YOU**'! he turned on his heal, and after wrenching the door open, looked back into the room '**YOU'LL REGRET THIS**'! then he was gone. Leaving dust motes spinning in his wake.
'Yeah. Yeah. Missing you already' muttered an unconvinced Farraday, as he waggled the "V" sign, made by the index and middle fingers, of his right hand, at his boss's departing back.

Chapter Nineteen

D. C. I. Trevor Hornby, pulled his car to the side
of the road. Leaving the engine running, he sat for a
moment, looking around to make sure that he wasn't
being watched. When he was happy, that his actions
would go unnoticed, the senior Policeman put his hand
into an inside pocket, of his tunic jacket, and took out his
own, personal mobile. Quickly, he dialled a number,
before placing the phone to his ear.
'It's Hornby'
'Did you succeed with your task'? asked a stern voice, at
the other end.
'Not exactly. No'
'What do you mean "Not exactly". Did you, or didn't
you'?
'No'
'If you can't do the job, then I'll send someone who can'!
'Don't you dare' : -
The signal went dead.
'HALLO. HALLO'? throwing the phone onto the
passenger seat, Hornby slammed the car into first gear,
accelerating hard into the traffic, causing several cars to
swerve. As the angry drivers swore and their horns
blared, Hornby sped off, to find somewhere to think.

Chapter Twenty

'Steve'?

'Yes Sarge'

'Can you meet me, at the cottage'?

'Yes, of course' then Lucas added 'Is there a problem'?

'No, I just want to have a chat, with Mr. Beecher'

'Ok' there was a short pause 'I can be there, in thirty to forty minutes'

'See you there' after replacing the telephone handset, Farraday looked at the note, that he had been given by Bridget.

Her neat hand writing said. *All requests for information, on the names you asked about, have been denied. They did **not**, come back as normal. I. E. "No information available" just "**Information denied**"*! now, alarm bells were ringing in Farraday's head. The contents of this note, and, D. C. I. Hornsby's request. No, his *order*, that he close the case immediately, meant only one thing. Somebody very powerful, wanted the case buried deep, and quickly. This knowledge, only served to spur him on. Picking up his car keys, he went to meet D. C. Steve Lucas.

Chapter Twenty One

Eustace Beecher, stood squinting through the crack between the dirty drapes, that covered the front room windows. For days now, if not weeks, he'd been expecting trouble, and when he'd heard the car doors slam outside, he'd picked up the Sten gun, that he'd carried with him, wherever he went, and headed for the window. Beecher gave out an almost audible sigh, when he recognised D. C. Lucas, although, he didn't recognise the man with him. He guessed, that he was more than likely, the Detective Constable's superior, which meant only one thing. They had found something out, and wanted to talk to him. Something that he couldn't let happen. Rushing into the hall, he stuffed his weapon into a ruck sack. Then after picking it up by the straps, headed for the back door, just managing to cover the but of the weapon, with the top flap of the back pack. There would be time to hide it properly, later. When he had gotten away.

A loud banging from the direction of the front door, made him freeze for a second, but only for a second, before he was moving again.
'Mr. Beecher'? shouted Farraday 'This is the Police. Open up'! the Detective banged on the door. When nothing happened, he slammed his closed fist on the wooden surface 'Go round the back Steve, just in case' he spoke in a whisper, before hammering on the front door again, and shouting 'Mr. Beecher. Open up'!
Lucas crept round to the back, just as Beecher was gently

closing the rear door. Eying the ruck sack with suspicion, Lucas stepped out, onto the over grown path.

'Going somewhere Mr. Beecher'?

The older man stopped, standing as if he had been turned to stone. Slowly, he turned to face the Policeman.

'What do you want'? he tried to keep his voice neutral, but was dismayed to hear a slight tremor in his words.

'Why don't you put the ruck sack down, then we can go inside and have a chat'?

Looking down at the bag in his left hand, Beecher said quietly 'I can't do that'!

'What, put the ruck sack down, or have a chat'?

'Either'

'Why'?

Looking at Lucas, his eyes showed just how afraid he was 'You'll want to take me in. And if you do that, I'll be dead within hours'!

'I don't understand. What are you afraid of'? Lucas had edged closer, by a few inches, and now he stopped, as he saw Beecher raise the ruck sack, so that he could place his right hand inside, just under the flap.

'I don't want to hurt you. Neither can I tell you anything. So just get out of my way'! Beecher really didn't, want to hurt anybody. He just wanted to live.

'Look' Lucas again managed to edge closer 'We can protect you from whoever it is, that is threatening you'

Beecher laughed. A sound that carried no humour 'You're just amateurs. You wouldn't be able to protect a bar of chocolate, from these people' tensing, as he saw Lucas move another step closer, he said 'So don't even try to kid yourself' his anguish evident in his voice. His words quietly spoken, as if to speak to loudly, would cause all his fears to become real 'Please just let me go.

69

If you don't, you'll not only put yourself in danger, but anybody else, who comes into contact with me'
'That's not possible' : - Lucas' words were cut off by Beecher's next action.
'I don't want to hurt you' he pointed the Sten gun at Lucas 'But I will, if I have to'!
Lucas swallowed hard, and for several long moments, stared at the barrel of the weapon, that was pointed at his chest 'Mr. Beecher'?
'Just do as I ask'! his finger tightened on the trigger, as his left hand came up to hold the magazine, which steadied the weapon.
'You'll have to kill us both'
Said a voice from behind him.
'So be it' raising the weapon slightly, he looked over his left shoulder 'If that's what it takes' then just as the Policeman thought that they had pushed their luck to far, Beecher lowered the submachine gun 'I can't do this' turning, he walked back into the house.
Both Detective's stood with their mouths open, for several seconds, before letting out long sighs. Then, they went to join Beecher.

'Is it safe'? Farraday nodded at the Sten.
'Not yet'! Beecher just sat staring into space.
'Will you do the honours, or shall I'? Farraday caught Lucas's anxious glance.
'Do you know how'? the older man finally lookcd at the Detective.
'No'
'Thought not'! lifting the Sten gun from the table, Beecher checked to make sure, that the safety catch was on, before pulling out the magazine. Finally, after taking

70

hold of the cocking lever, he checked to make sure that the firing chamber was clear. Gently placing the weapon on the table, he looked first at Farraday, then Lucas, before holding up his arms, wrists together 'Go on then, slap them on'!

Farraday sat down opposite him 'I don't think that will be necessary, do you'?

Beecher frowned 'I don't understand. I thought that you had come to arrest me'?

'That may be on the cards' nodding at the submachine gun, he needed to say no more 'But what I'm interested in, is why you thought we were going to arrest you, and why you need that'? he pointed at the old weapon 'For protection'?

'I can't tell you'

Lucas lent forward, his elbows resting on the table 'I think you had better start talking, or, you're going to end up in even more trouble'! Lucas was shaking, not, as he hoped that Beecher would think, anger, but with the after shock, of having a gun pointed at him.

'If you believe that this, good cop bad cop, routine, is going to wear me down' : -

Farraday held up a hand 'Hey' smiling, he looked at Lucas 'Cool it Steve' then, looking at Beecher, his voice became harsh 'How did you expect D. C. Lucas to react, after you'd stuck a gun in his face'?

'I was aiming at his chest actually'

'**Shut up**'! snapped Farraday

Beecher looked angrily at the Detective Sergeant.

'Let me tell you, how this is going to go'

'If you think' : - Beecher started to rise.

Farraday slammed his fist down onto the table, making both the older man and Lucas, jump.

'SIT DOWN'!

Beecher did as he had been ordered.

'Now, you've got just one more chance to explain what's going on'

Beecher opened his mouth, to offer an argument.

'Before you start to say anything, I want you to listen to what I have to say'! he waited for a second, or so, to give Beecher a chance to take in, what he had just said. Also it gave him a moment to clear his mind, to enable him to accept and hopefully, understand, what he was about to say 'I have no doubt, that you are in serious danger. However, you must understand that you *will,* answer my questions'!

'And If I don't'?

'I believe I'm being watched' he was pleased to see the alarm, in the old mans eyes 'And if you don't tell me what I need to know, I will have no problem with letting the people who are after you, know exactly where you are'!

'You dirty bastard'! Beecher spoke through clenched teeth, his jaw muscles worked, as his teeth ground together.

'That may be true, but people are getting murdered all around me, and I want to know why. If that means I have to use dirty tricks, to get what I want, then I will'

'Sarge'? warned a shocked Lucas.

'SHUT UP'! Farraday snapped.

Lucas wasn't sure what was going on, but he knew Farraday well enough to understand, that whatever it was, that he was trying to achieve, was important enough for him to act out of character.

'Don't you understand' Beecher was desperate 'If I tell you what I know, then it'll not only be me that gets silenced'!

'I've had threats made against me' : -

'What'? Lucas couldn't believe his ears.

'Nothing specific, but I was left in no doubt, that I would suffer in some way, if I didn't bury this case' grimacing as he looked at Beecher, he carried on 'I won't stop investigating the murders' looking hard at Beecher, his words heavy with hidden meaning, he added 'And unless you tell me what I'm up against, or to be more precise, who. My guess is, that I won't be alive long enough to finish my job' the room went quiet, as each of the three men thought about what had just been said. After about five minutes, Beecher broke the silence.

'Ok, I'll tell you what I know'

Chapter Twenty Two

Sitting back in his chair, Beecher gave each of the Detectives, a hard stare before letting out a long despairing sigh.

'This place' he squinted at the kitchen walls, as if he could see beyond them 'Doesn't belong to me' a cheerless laugh, escaped his throat 'Never has, never will'

'Who *does,* it belong to then'? Lucas asked impatiently.

'Our beloved government. Although I doubt that anybody, in the hierarchy, knows anything about it. I don't suppose many people do' almost under his breath, he added 'I suppose it's been that way for years'

'Why do you come hear then'?

Beecher looked at Farraday 'Two reasons. Firstly, I come looking for clues. Secondly, I come when I feel the need to be safe'

'I don't understand. Clues to what'? the senior Detectives eyes shone, with an inner light.

'And safe from who'? Lucas was also becoming intensely interested.

'All in good time' the old man smiled 'I promise you, that all your questions will be answered' licking his lips nervously, he sat deep in thought, trying to get the facts straight before he started telling his story.

Farraday and Lucas, glanced at each other, both impatient for information. But at the same time, content to let Beecher take his time.

'You lot today' Beecher snorted in derision 'Think that

Cloning is a modern abomination. Believe me, it isn't'
both Detectives looked nervous and stunned, all at the
same time.

'During the second World War, I trained as a
Commando. From just fourteen, I was taught to shoot,
blow things up and I was also taught to kill, in every
conceivable way. When I was eighteen. Myself and those
who had trained with me, were unleashed on the enemy'
a cold icy blast of memory, chilled his blood and he gave
an involuntary shudder 'In those days, it wasn't always
clear, exactly who, the enemy was. There were no signs
pointing to a person, saying *This man, or this woman, is
the enemy"*, and so, sometimes the people we were sent
to kill, looked just like ordinary members of the public.
We never argued of course, because we trusted our
superiors completely' he gave another sour chuckle 'That
was our first mistake'

'But I don't understand. What could the war possibly
have to do with Cloning'? Farraday was starting to lose
the thread, of what the man before him, was saying.

'Times were desperate, and people were trying all sorts
of mad ideas, in an effort to even the odds. To become
better than the enemy. But very few of those ideas
actually worked. Then, one man came up with the idea,
of replacing high ranking officials with a duplicate.
Everybody has heard, of how Churchill and Hitler, used
actors to impersonate them. Well, just imagine, if we
could actually have positioned our own agents, in the
place of certain leaders. The war could have been over in
months, if not weeks. There was of course several
problems. Finding perfect Doppelgangers, was unlikely,
and plastic surgery was only in its infancy. So, a think
tank of the countries top scientists, was founded. From

the group came a plan. They would breed replicas of the most important enemy leaders, picked out as targets. They gave the idea a name. It was to be called *"GHOSTING"*. This in itself, bought up not only scientific problems, but also, biological, ethical and moral dilemmas. How do you breed an exact replica, for a start. And, if you did get that far, how could you make the replacement age fast enough, to look like the leader, that he, or she, was supposed to take the place of. Then, once they had gotten to the correct age, how did you stop the premature ageing process from going further'? Beecher shook his head, as if the memories were becoming to much for him to bear 'Anyway, that side of it, is well above my head' looking over his shoulder, Beecher stared out through the grimy window, it wasn't going to be long before it started to get dark 'Me and the lads, had been working on special operations for the S. O. E. and S. I. S.

'Who on earth are the S. O. E. and S. I. S.'?

Beecher smiled a secret smile 'They were the forerunner of todays Secret Services. The Special Operations Executive and Special Intelligence Services' a small chuckle rose up from his chest 'Mind you, at the time, they were just a hotchpotch mixture, of inexperienced hopefuls' fidgeting, he tried to get comfortable 'Anyway, for several months, towards the end of Forty Three, we were billeted at a house on Exmoore' he shook his head 'Not so much a house as a fortress, hiding a laboratory. Our job of course, was to guard it'

'This is all very interesting, but what has it got to do with what's happening today'?

'Haven't you put it together yet'?

'No'

76

'The labs, were where they ran the Ghosting experiments. From what we heard, things weren't going to well. That was until an agent from S. O. E. found out about Doctor Morrela Shlicke'

'I take it, that she was a German scientist'?

'Oh yes. And she was the key to gaining their goal, of producing a Cloned, enemy leader' stopping, Beecher stood up. After massaging his buttocks, he lent against one of the dilapidated cupboards 'Our job was to go and liberate her' he chuckled to himself 'Liberate. Kidnap, is a more appropriate word'

'Are you telling us, that this Morrela Shlicke, is the woman that used to live here'?

'Give the man a goldfish' there was no sarcasm in the old soldiers voice.

'But why would the people who had wanted her so badly, want her dead. If she *is,* dead'? this tale of intrigue, was starting to get a bit complicated for Lucas.

'Accountability'! he looked at the two Detectives, who just returned his glance, with blank expressions 'If there's no evidence, then those who had ordered the experiments to take place, can't be held, *accountable*'!

'I see' Farraday nodded 'But why so late after the war'?

'The experiments never came to fruition. not that is, until after the war and well into the fifties. Obviously, it was to late to have any effect on the outcome of the Second World War. But by then, the west was having trouble with the Russians. Once they'd gotten what they wanted, from the scientists, most of them disappeared. Only Schlicke, proved to be more of a problem. She was tough, and the men that were sent to neutralise her, weren't women killers. They were tough, but not cold hearted'

'Was it you'? Farraday asked quietly.

'What'? he frowned 'Who was sent to kill her'? Farraday nodded his confirmation 'No' sitting down again, he sighed 'Buy this time, we, me and the men that I worked with, had our own problems'

'What sort of problems'? Lucas could guess, but he wanted to know for sure.

'Like most of the scientists, we had out lived our usefulness and had become an, *embarrassment*'

'So they tried to kill you'? Beecher nodded '*All,* of you'?

'All but one'

'Oh, and who was that'?

'A man named Agent Arrow'!

Chapter Twenty Three

'What did Agent Arrow do'?

'He was the marksman of the group'

'So he was used to what, take out those that got in the way'?

'Not at first. He was used, when needed on our missions, but eventually, he got a taste for it, and became an S. O. E. assasin'

'And it's him, that's after you'?

'I believe so, yes'?

'But how come you weren't killed, years ago'?

'Four of us escaped'

'Four'?

'Yes'

'And what happened to the other three'?

'You found one in the church. One was dug up in the grounds of the fort and the last one, was Gregory Lockhart'

'Mr. Lockhart, was one of your merry group'?

'He was'

'So how come, the one in the grounds of the fort, didn't live so long'?

'He was unlucky, that's all'

'And another thing. If he was murdered, why weren't the rest of you found and killed'? Lucas was really starting, to get interested now.

'He was killed miles away, we found his body and brought it here. We couldn't, unfortunately have a proper funeral, so we did what we could'

'The man in the church. Morgan Whitaker. What were the marks on his arm for, the numbers that were tattooed near the underside, of his left wrist'?

'It was done, to put people off his scent'! a dark cloud crossed his face 'Not that it worked' Beecher grumbled to himself.

'I take it that Hilda Lockhart, knew about her husbands past'?

'She must have known some of it, but possibly not everything'

'She knew enough, to point us in this direction' Beecher smiled 'She knew I was here'

'She'd seen you'?

'No. After Gregory's death, I introduced myself'

'But why are you here'?

'As I said. I'm looking for clues'

'Clues'?

'Yes' Beecher glanced out the window, and saw that full darkness was only minutes away.

'Can you be a bit more specific'?

'When doctor Shlicke lived here, she told Gregory that she had hidden some evidence, of what she had been doing, in and around this cottage'

'And you've spent what, twenty years, trying to find these clues'?

'No, only about two or three'

'And have you found out anything'? Beecher shook his head 'And why should we believe you'?

'Do you think, I'd still be here, if I'd found out anything'?

'No, I suppose not'

'And if I was such a bad bloke, do you think that I would have risked getting arrested, by not shooting you'?

Farraday and Beecher relaxed, then smiled at each other.
'True. I suppose' Farraday conceded.
'I thought you'd been here for years'? Lucas questioned
Beecher.
'I lied'
'And you got upset, because we didn't believe you' the
senior Detective chided.
'I know. But sometimes, a man has to do, what a man has
to do'!
'So, what happens to you now'?
'That largely depends on you' Beecher raised an
eyebrow.
'There's no easy answers. But a lot of questions. So, I
guess I'll have to trust my gut instincts'
'Must be a big instinct' Lucas joked.
'**Shut it**'! Farraday shot a warning look at his friend.
'As I was saying' again he glanced at Lucas 'I'm going to
trust my instinct, too let you go'
'And will you'?
'Yes'!
'Sarge'?
'**What**'?
'Do you think, that this is a good idea'? the younger
Policeman, could see his career going down the toilet.
'Have you got a better one'? Farraday asked quietly.
'Yes I' Lucas paused 'No'! he finally agreed.
'I didn't think so' Farraday looked back at Beecher
'Where will you go'?
'Ask me no questions' Beecher said mysteriously.
'And we can't tell anybody, where you've gone, if we
don't know' Farrady finished for him.
'Something like that'
'I don't believe this'! Lucas stood up, pointing angrily at

Farrday 'You're going to just let him walk away, as if nothing has happened'?

'Steve' Farraday looked at the other Detective 'What else can I do'?

'**Arrest him**'! his voice had risen to a shout.

'**No**'!

'Excuse me. I *am* still here, you know' Beecher grumpily butted in.

'**SHUT IT**'! shouted Lucas.

'Steve, will you calm down'!

'**NO**'! Lucas spoke between clenched teeth '**I will *not*, calm down**'!

'You know as well as I do, that if we take him in, we'll be signing his death warrant'?

'How is he going to get killed, in a Police cell. In a Police station, crawling with Police'?

'Steve'? Farraday said patiently 'Sometimes, for an intelligent and experienced Policeman, you can be very stupid and nieve'!

Lucas put his face, just a few inches away from Farraday's. In a voice that was low and full of menace, he said '**For an experienced and intelligent Policeman, *and*'** he added for good measure '**My best friend**' he swallowed '**You can be a complete and total arsehole**'! straightening up, he looked down at the senior Detective '**You either back me up. Or keep out of my way**'!

'**HOW DARE YOU TALK**' : - Farraday shook with rage.

'Gentlemen'? Beecher spoke quietly but firmly.

A mechanical click, made them both look in the general direction, of the other man.

'There is no way, that I'm going to go with you, to a Police station. So get used to the idea'!

'We've been through this once already. There is no way that you would kill even one of us. Let alone both of us'!
'Who said anything about, *killing*. A bullet in the leg, can be very disabling'
'**You wouldn't dare**'! Lucas wasn't quite so sure.
'Try me'! slowly, he raised the Sten gun.
'So, what is this, a Mexican stand off'? Lucas took a step forward.
Beecher slowly shook his head, and took a tighter grip on his weapon. Lucas took another cautious step. There was a flash from the muzzle of the submachine gun, and the room was filled with the roar, of the single shot. The air filled with the smell of gunpowder. Lucas fell to the floor, grasping the thigh of his left leg. Farraday stood up. Beecher turned to face him.
'Don't'!
'I can't let you' : -
'You have no choice'
'I can't just stand back. Not now'
'As I said. You have no choice'
'Really'?
'Your friend needs you, and you'll be no good to him, if I have to shoot you as well'!
'You wouldn't'?
Beecher raised his eyebrows.
'Let him go Hector' Lucas groaned.
'What'?
'**Just bloody do it Hector, and don't be such an arse**'!

Chapter Twenty Four

'You've changed your tune'! Farraday was angry and
confused.

'What do you want me to say, go on then, have a go. If I
do that, all that will happen, is that you'll get shot'!
Farrady looked back at their captor 'Will I'?

'Get shot'? the older man nodded 'If you get in my way.
You'll leave me no choice'

'So what happens now'? Farrday knelt beside his friend,
who was trying to stop his leg from bleeding.

'Here, take this' he handed Lucas a folded handkerchief
'Hold that against the wound, and press it as hard as you
can' Lucas gave the creased square, of striped material, a
worried look 'It's ok, it is clean'

'I go, is what happens next' Beecher glanced out of the
window, into the darkness 'But I'll keep in touch'

'What good will that do'? snapped Farrady angrily.

'For one thing. I know who Agent Arrow is. You don't. I
also have this' he held up his faithful Sten Gun.

'How will we contact you'? Lucas' face was screwed up
in pain.

'You won't. I'll contact you'!

'Oh, how very Secret Service' mumbled Farriday,
snotily.

'Fine, you have it your way. But I'll be around'

'**Just go**'! Farraday wanted him out of there, before he
changed his mind.

'Ok, but remember. I'll be watching'! with a last look
around, he quickly opened the back door, stepping out

into the night.

Farraday took his mobile phone, from his pocket. After dialling a number and waiting for a few seconds, he spoke when the ring was finally answered 'Ambulance please'

'Is it true'? Lucas looked at Farraday closely.

'What'? the older Detective asked absentmindedly.

'You getting threatened'?

'Is it important'?

'Yes'

'Why'?

'Just tell me'!

'Hornby asked me to close this case' scoffing, he corrected himself 'Well actually, he told me to "Bury it"'!

'What did you say'?

'What do you think I said'?

'No'? Lucas ventured.

'Damn right'!

'Then, what happened'?

'Oh I don't know, some loose remark about me regretting my actions'

'Are you worried'?

'Nah' he smiled 'Well, not much, anyway'

'Sarge'? Lucas said, after a short silence.

'What'?

'I have a bad feeling about this'

'It must be the lack of blood'

'I'm serious Hector'! his voice was loosing its strength.

'So am I'

'Look' swallowing, Lucas fought to stay conscious 'I really *am* serious' his voice had become high pitched, with frustration.

'Ok, ok, calm down'!
'Just listen will you'!

Chapter Twenty Five

'I have something to say and I want you to listen, without interrupting me, because I don't know if I'll have the strength to finish, if you do' Lucas grimaced.

'This sounds heavy'

'No not really. I just think that it's important'

'Ok then, fire away'

'Some months ago, I was out with some friends, and I went to see a palm reader' he smiled 'Just for a laugh, you understand' Lucas saw the look of consternation, on his friends face 'There's no need to look like that'!

'What'? smiled Farraday.

'Never mind' time was short 'And she told me things, that she had no way of knowing. On top of all this, she gave me a warning'

'And you believed her'?

'Yes'

'So what was this warning'?

'She told me, that I was going to look death in the face, and that I would need somewhere safe, to run to'

'And so what did you do'?

'I went and found myself, somewhere safe'! his eyes started to close.

'Steve'! Farraday gave the young Detective a shake.

'Hmm'?

'Where is it then'?

'What'?

'This "Somewhere safe to run to"'?

'Up in the hills, above the village' with a fading voice,

Lucas continued 'I remember my grandad, talking about a place that he used during the war'

'But there aren't any houses up there' Farraday had started to wonder, if Lucas was becoming delirious.

'It's not a house'

'What is it then'?

'It's, or at least was, an arms dump for the Home Guard'

'What! You mean somewhere to hid their broom handles'? Farraday asked sarcastically.

'No. This place is full of stuff'

'So, how will it help you'?

'Not me. Us' he smiled weakly at Farraday 'You and me'

'Why would *I,* need a place to hide'? he wore a frown

'Unless this fortune teller, told you that I was in danger'?

'No, of course not, but you said that you were being watched'!

'I did'

'And so, if this turns bad, you've at least got somewhere to go'

'True' Farraday nodded 'And where exactly, is this hidey-hole'?

Lucas dropped his voice to little more than a whisper 'If you take the main footpath up into the hills, you'll eventually come to a big old oak, standing on its own' swallowing, Lucas tried to moistened his dry throat 'If you stand with your back to it, and face east, you'll see a clump of brambles about five hundred yards away. If you go to the back of those brambles, you'll find a hole. Crawl into that hole and follow it to the centre. In the middle, under the soil, which is about four or five inches deep, you will find a trap door' putting his hand, into his trousers pocket, he fished out a bunch of keys 'You'll need this, to open the padlock' he took a key of off the metal ring, that it was attached to. Reaching out, he gave it to Farraday.

'What about you'?

'I have a spare key'

'What's this place like, then'?

'It's basically, a large concrete box in the ground'

'Damp, I suppose'?

'No, it's as dry as a, a, a. Well, it's dry' wiping the back of his hand, across his eyes, his voice dropped lower than a whisper 'It has all the mod cons. Bottled water, camping stove and bunk beds' his head dropped, until his chin rested on his chest 'Oh yeah' a little chuckle echoed in his throat 'And a couple of riffles' Lucas's eyes slowly closed, as he dropped into unconsciousness.

'What'? Farraday gave his friend a shake, but he was too deeply under, to respond.

Chapter Twenty Six

Farraday stood with his back to the old oak tree. Facing east. Just as his friend had told him to do. There, in the distance, about five hundred yards, or so, in front of him, nestled a clump of brambles. Just as promised. Looking around him, Farraday made sure that he was alone, before making his way to the back of the tangle, of blackberry bushes. With a last glance along the foot path, the Detective got down onto his hands and knees. Pushing a loose runner, out of the way, he peered into the dark tunnel. After a second, of cautious reflection, he crawled slowly into the deepening gloom. The further that he went, the darker it became. Until, by the time he had reached the centre, the Detective was cosseted in total darkness. Taking a small torch from his coat pocket, he aimed the bright beam onto the ground. Using his hands, he dug into the loose, dry, soil. Just as he was beginning worry that, perhaps, he was digging in the wrong place, the fingers of his right hand scrapped along something hard. After five minutes of fast soil clearing, a metal trapdoor had, finally, been uncovered. Farraday sat back on his haunches, surveying his handy work, brushing the last of the dust from the padlock, he placed the key, that Lucas had given him, into the keyhole and gave it a twist. There was a satisfying clunk, as the lock opened. Gritting his teeth, Farraday lifted the sheet of steel that guarded the entrance, to the interior. Praying that the hinges wouldn't make a noise. With a sigh of relief, the metal door opened all the way, without so much as a whimper. By the light of his torch, he found the ladder, that would take him down into the subterranean chamber. Slowly, and with great caution, he climbed down, one rung at a time. Stopping after about four feet, low enough, so that he wouldn't hit his head, the Detective closed the trapdoor, before continuing with his descent.

Swinging the narrow beam of his hand torch, around the area in which he stood, Farraday tried to get some idea of the size of the chamber. However, the torch that he had bought with him, was far to small to be of any real help. So, looking around in the hope of finding something better, he smiled when he saw what he was looking for. Carefully he made his way over to a small table, that he assumed, would be used by the owners, to eat their meals. Taking a box of matches, that lay beside the lantern, Farraday gently turned a knob at the side, and heard a satisfying hiss of gas, as it escaped from the nozzle inside the filament. Carefully, he placed his burning match to the mantle. The room was bathed in bright light.

Turning off his torch, the puny beam lost against the powerful light, from the gas lamp, the Detective took a look around. What he noticed, with hard to explain delight, was an Aladdin's cave of equipment. Enough to last two people, many months. As he walked around the chamber, he gained some impression of its size. Although, with so many ammunition boxes stacked against the wall, it was hard to gauge the true dimensions with any great accuracy, he guessed that he was in a. What should it be called? Room? Chamber? Or perhaps, Dungeon. Chamber, seemed to be the best name. So, he calculated that the "Chamber", was the best part of, thirty feet long, seven feet high and fifteen feet wide. The walls were brick, while the floor was made of poured concrete. The ceiling looked like it had been constructed, by putting large reinforced concrete slabs together, on top of the walls, so that they spanned the structure. For the first time, Farraday noticed, that there was a slight draught running length ways, through the chamber, which lead him to believe that somehow, the people responsible for building this underground hideaway, had managed to install good ventilation. Hence the reason for it being so dry. As he paced slowly around the room, he touched the many cardboard boxes, standing neatly against the walls. Noting, that the majority of them, held food stuff. Both tinned and in powder form. Stepping up to the table, he took hold of the lanterns handle and carrying it with him, he ventured to the far end of the concrete room, where he noticed, what he believed to be a work bench, which stretched across the entire wall, at that end of the chamber. What was revealed to him, by the light from the gas lamp, was a well laid out area, in which sat radio receivers, frequency scanners and dozens of packs of batteries. What held his attention the most, however, were the items hanging on a wrack, that had been securely bolted to the brickwork. Lifting his right hand, Farraday touched the lowest item. Only then, did he get a waft of what he assumed, was gun oil. Four rifles sat comfortably and safely, before him. Two Lee Enfield mark ones, with high powered telescopic sights, attached, and two snub nose Lee Enfield's. All four weapons looked brand new. Farraday noticed, what he assumed, were boxes of ammunition, stacked on the right hand side, of the work bench. Placing the hissing lantern, on the wooden surface, the Detective grabbed hold of the first metal container. Lifting the latch, which held the lid safely closed, he then pulled it up and back, releasing the top, so that he could peer inside. His assumption had been correct. Inside, lay dozens of .303in calibre bullets. 'Wow' Farraday muttered quietly, as he gently ran his fingers along one of the rounds. Slowly and quietly, he closed the lid on the ammunition box, almost as if he believed that, to close the lid too harshly, would somehow set the bullets off. Or if he made to much noise, someone may well hear him.

Putting the lantern back, where he had found it, Farraday took a last look around, before reluctantly leaving.

Chapter Twenty Seven

Ever since the body had been found, in the grounds of the old fort, the work of turning the derelict war horse into a home, had been stopped completely. But now that the Police had given him the all clear, Monty had managed, through Harry "Duke" Elington, his Site Manager, to get everybody back and working. Monty had very little contact with the people working on the site, his main channel of communication was Duke. From what he had seen so far, the Site Manager was a hard, but fair task master. As promised, his office on the roof of the old fort, was one of the first of the many projects to be finished. Along with the roof repairs, and the replacement windows. Looking around at his office, a satisfied smile slowly overtook his features, finally becoming a full beam. The builders had done, both him and themselves, proud. They had not only, made his office somewhere in which to work, as promised, they had done their work, to such a high degree, that he had asked them to carry on and finish the decorating, and fix up the lighting. Now, all he needed was for his furniture to arrive, which was hopefully going to be this afternoon, and he would be able to get back to work. Looking out through the curved window, which took up the whole of one wall, he drank in the magnificent view of the river Thames. As he watched the river flow by, he became almost mesmerised by the rippling surface. It wasn't until a flash of light caught the corner of his eye, that he was able to pull himself away, from his river induced trance.

Looking to the left, he tried to see what it was that had reflected the sun. For several minutes, he stood looking out across the marshes. Until, finally, he saw what he believed to be a man, in a clump of bulrushes.

'Hmm' Monty chuckled to himself 'Twitcher'

His smile slowly faded, as he remembered that this wasn't the first time, that he thought he was being watched. Shaking his head, he said to himself.

'Ghosts. This place must be full of them'

By six o'clock that evening, the people who were supplying his new office equipment, had delivered it, installed it and left. Now, all that was needed for him to do, was turn on his computer and check that he had installed everything correctly, including his wireless broadband connection.

With a hesitant finger, he pressed the "ON" switch. To his great surprise, after just a few minutes, everything was working perfectly, even the internet connection.

'Great'! Monty grinned like the proverbial, Cheshire cat 'Now I can get some real work done'!

Sitting at his computer, he flexed the fingers of both hands, almost as if he were a concert pianist getting ready to give the performance of his life. Monty was just about to start typing, when a warning "Ping", informed him, that he had email. Clicking on the email icon, he waited for the message to appear on the screen. When it did, it caused more than just confusion.

"YOU HAVE SOMETHING I WANT"!

Thinking that it was someone playing a silly game, or one of those purvey messages, that he'd heard about, he simply deleted it. However, a second later, the message was back.

"YOU HAVE SOMETHING I WANT"!!!!!
Quickly, he again hit the delete button.
"YOU HAVE SOMETHING I WANT !!!! IGNORE THIS MESSAGE AT YOU PERIL"!!!
Looking for the address of the sender, he was amazed, when he couldn't find one.
'That's not possible' he mumbled to himself. Thinking quickly, he set about answering the message. Not sure if he was doing the right thing.
"Who are you, and what do you want"?
"YOU HAVE 7 DAYS, TOO GIVE ME WHAT I WANT"!
Monty's fingers flew over the keys, as he typed "I don't know what it is, that you think I have, belonging to you"!
"YOU WILL, WHEN YOU FIND IT"!
Monty had had enough **"GO AWAY AND DON'T COME BACK"**!!!!! he typed angrily.
"THE CLOCK IS TICKING. YOU HAVE 7 DAYS, TOO GIVE ME WHAT IS MINE"!!!
"And if I don't"? sweat had started to bead, on his forehead.
No answer came, for several seconds. Then came the two word reply.
"YOU DIE"!!!! nothing else, just those two chilling words.
Monty sat staring at his monitor, for several seconds, before closing his email. What was he going to do? He had no idea what the person, or persons, wanted. Or even *if,* the messages had been meant as a joke. What ever happened, he wasn't laughing.

Opening a draw, on the right side of his desk, Monty took out a large leather bound address book. After finding the telephone number of his internet provider, he entered the digits into his mobile.

'Good evening. This is UK World Internet. My name is Brad. How may I help you'? said a young polite voice, at the other end.

'Err'? Monty started falteringly 'Yes. My name is Monty Barrington-Wright. I think that I've just had a malicious email.

'I see' the young man had become very business like 'May I have your email address and the telephone number that you use'?

After Monty had given the requested information, he waited.

'Ok sir. May I have the last four digits, of your credit card, please'?

Again Monty waited.

'Sorry about that, Mr. Barrington-Wright'

'That's ok'

'Thank you sir' there was a seconds wait, and then Brad spoke 'Can you tell me the nature, of the email, and if possible, the wording it contained'?

'Of course' Monty told him exactly, what had happened.

'Ok sir. Thank you' Brad cleared his throat 'As you probably know sir, we and the other internet providers, take any non-acceptable conduct, very seriously and we will take whatever actions are necessary, to stop such things occurring' it was evident, in the preoccupied way that Brad was talking, that he was doing something else, at the same time as he was speaking to Monty 'Did you save the email, or delete it'?

'I'm afraid that I deleted it'

'Not to worry' the line went quiet for a moment, or two 'While we've been talking, I've been having a look at your email, from this end. But at the moment, I can't find anything. So what I'll do, is give you an incident number,

97

so that if you get any more problem emails, like the one you've just reported, please save them and call us back, and give this number to the person that you speak to'
'Ok'
'With luck, this won't happen again. However, if it does, we'll put a tail on your email, and see if we can find out who's sending them. Once that's done, we will put a stop to them causing you any more such problems'
'Thank you' after taking down the incident number, Monty shut the flap on his mobile phone. He felt relieved at having done something, and, he had to admit, he felt safer. However, his feelings of security, wouldn't last long.

Chapter Twenty Eight

Monty had spent, what was left of the evening, working. The earlier fear forgotten. Finally, a little after one o'clock in the morning, Monty went to bed. Well, if it could be called a bed. It was actually a camp bed, in one of the rooms, that had been tidied up.

Six thirty, the next morning, saw him back at his desk, holding a steaming mug of tea. Tapping the mouse, he stopped the screen saver from crossing the flat screen. The first thing that he saw, was the flashing email icon. Nervously, he moved the pointer over the "In box" and clicked.

"Hallo" said the email.

Monty, just sat looking at the single word. Sweat starting to bead on his top lip. Looking for the address of the person who had sent the electronic message, he started to get even more afraid, when he couldn't see who the sender was.

"Who are you"? nervously, he waited for a reply.

"*YOU HAVE JUST 6 DAYS*"!!!

"**GO TO HELL**"!!! after hitting the send button, he waited.

Nothing happened. Just when he thought this problem had gone away. A new message came in.

"*IF YOU DON'T GIVE ME WHAT I WANT, I'LL SEE YOU THERE*"!!!

"I don't know what you want"!!!! "You'll need to tell me what it is, I'm supposed too have, that belongs to you"!!!

"*We need to meet*"

"**NO**"!!!

"*YOU AREN'T IN A POSITION TO ARGUE*"!!!

"**NO**"!!!

"*If you want to save your life, you have no choice*"!!!

"Where"?

"*I'll contact you*"

"When"? nothing happened "**WHEN**"? still nothing "**ANSWER ME. DAMN YOU**"!!! again no answer. Monty slammed both fists down on the desktop, the vibrations causing the tea in his mug, to spill over the lip. Picking up his mobile, Monty gave himself a moment to calm down, before dialling the number of his internet provider. In just two rings, the phone was answered. 'Good morning. This is the help line of UK World Internet. My name is Sandra. How may I help you'? Monty waited patiently, for the woman's singsong voice to finish, then said 'I have an incident number' 'Ok, sir. May I take the number'? she waited while Monty read it out to her 'Ok, am I talking to Mr. Monty Barrington-Wright'? 'Yes' 'Will you just confirm your identity information, for me please'? Monty read out the requested data, his voice almost a monotone 'Thank you' after a few seconds, the woman came back on the line 'I see that you've had a malicious email. Is that correct'? 'Yes' 'May I assume, that you've had another one'? 'Yes' 'Ok, sir. If you will just bear with me for a moment'? Monty could hear the tapping of keys. Then, Sandra's voice almost made him jump 'I see that Brad took your initial call' it was a statement, not a question. So Monty said nothing 'Would you like to talk to me, or Brad. I've checked, and he's on duty this morning'?

'Oh. Err, Brad' he added quietly, as he felt a bit guilty 'If that's ok'?

'I'll just put you through sir'

Monty took it, that it must have been ok, as Sandra's singsong voice never changed.

'Hallo Mr. Barrington-Wright. This is Brad'

'Hi Brad'

'I see that you've had some more trouble'!

'Yes' Monty spoke quietly, almost as if he feared, that he was doing something wrong, and if he spoke in to loud a voice, he may well get caught.

'Ok. Let me just have a quick look' again Monty caught the sound of tapping keys 'I'm just checking on the results, from last time. Then we can chat about the new problem. Will that be ok Mr. Barrington-Wright'?

'Yes, that'll be fine. Oh and Brad'?

'Yes sir'? answered Brad, in an absentminded voice.

'Please call me Monty'

'Ok, Monty' several minutes passed, before Brad spoke again 'Monty'?

'Yes'?

'It would appear, that our technicians have drawn a blank' his voice carried a mixture of concern, and confusion 'Which is a bit strange' the line crackled 'Let me just have a look at this. Arr, here we are'?

'Have you found something'?

'I'm just looking at your latest email' Monty could hear the frown, in Brad's voice 'I don't know how this has happened, but it would appear, that there is no senders address'

'Is that possible'? for a moment, Monty had stopped

feeling afraid, because his natural inquisitiveness had taken over.

'In theory. No'

'So how have they done it'?

'I have no idea'

'What do we do now, then'?

'I think the best thing for me to do, is try to follow the emails trail, and see where that leads. Unfortunately, that could take some time. So would you mind, if I phoned you back'?

'No. Not at all'

'Please don't worry, if you don't hear from me, for a day or two, I will definitely let you know how I get on. Oh, and one last thing'!

'Hmm'?

'Is it ok, if I keep an eye on your emails, just in case you get any more troublesome ones'?

'Of course'

'Ok then, Monty, I'll say goodbye, for know'

The line went dead, and just before Monty took the phone away from his ear, he thought he heard a second click. Almost as if someone had been eavesdropping. Shaking his head, he sat staring at the tiny LED that was flashing on his mobile, that told him, the battery was empty and needed charging.

Sighing, Monty stood up. Any thought of work, having gone from his head, he decided to go for a walk instead. "Perhaps" he thought "The fresh air, would do him good".

Standing on the river bank, a light breeze gently gliding across his skin, the fresh salty aroma of the air, flowing into his lungs. As he breathed deeply, in an attempt to clear the angst, that had started to work its way through his system. Monty couldn't help but wonder, if he hadn't in fact, dreamt, what had been happening to him, over the last couple of days. This was after all, modern Britain, things like this didn't happen here. If it hadn't been for the body, that had been found in the grounds of the fort, and the murders that he had heard about, then he might have been able to believe, what he had just tried to tell himself.

Monty was just turning to retrace his steps back home, when something hit him on the back of the head. Just before everything went black, he thought he heard a sardonic chuckle.

Chapter Twenty Nine

'Errrhm'? Monty groaned. Trying to move his head, he started to feel sick, so he went back to letting his chin rest on his chest. He then tried to move his arms, confusion flooding his mind, when he couldn't get his limbs to respond. Suddenly, he felt very afraid, perhaps he'd had some sort of stroke. Yes! That was it. That's what the throbbing in his head meant, and there were other things. He was sure that he had gone blind.

Reason started to seep back into his mind, to counter his feelings of panic. Slowly, it became obvious why he could not see. He was somewhere dark. This became obvious, when out of the corner of his eye, there was just visible, a shaft of sunlight, slanting through a hole high up in one of the walls. As his senses started to clear, Monty realised that his arms wouldn't move, due to the fact that they had been tied.

'Why'? at first,Monty didn't realise that he had spoken 'Help' his voice croaked 'Hel' : -

A flame flickered in a far corner, off to his right, cutting off his words, as if the yellow light was as sharp as a razor blade. A fraction of a second later, the flare was replaced by the red orange glow, of a burning cigarette end.

'HELP'! this time, Monty's voice had more power in it. 'I really should give these up you know' the strangers voice, had a surreal effect on Monty. Due, no doubt, in part, to the fact that he couldn't see the owner.

'HELLLP'!

'No point in wasting your breath, nobody can hear you' a humourless chuckle escaped the man hidden in the shadows, and bounced around the walls 'Lovely echo, don't you think'? when Monty gave no answer, the stranger continued 'Gives our little party, an air of' he hesitated, as he searched for an appropriate word 'Hostility. Oh yeah, and danger, of course'
'Who are you and what do you want'?
'Are yes' he took a draw on his cigarette, Monty could see the end glowing even brighter 'The most asked questions, of those in danger'
If he kept using the word, *danger,* to scare Monty, then it was having the desire effect.
'Just give me a straight answer'! his voice had the slightest quiver to it. The first sign of his rising panic.
'You should learn to be more patient, my boy' again, came that annoying chuckle 'Isn't it funny, how one persons voice, can cause an echo, while another's won't'?
'Hilarious' Monty mumbled under his breath.
'In answer to your first question. *"Who am I"?* that question isn't as easy to answer, as it would seem. So let me put it this way. My job doesn't have a title. But every country has people like me. Persons, who are dedicated to their Home Land, and who will do anything to protect its safety and sanctity' he smile to himself, a gesture unseen by his prisoner 'I suppose that I could be called a, *Night Watchman,* or a, *Mister fix it.* Even, I suppose, a government, *Vacuum Cleaner.* Someone who gets rid of all the dirt, without hiding it under the carpet' he took another drag on his cigarette, before dropping it onto the floor, and crushing it under the sole of his right, hand made leather shoe. The grit making a scratching sound,

105

as he twisted his foot 'I could go on, but I think you get the picture'! he coughed to clear the phlegm from his throat, the last remnants of a nasty cold, that had been bugging him for weeks 'To answer your second question. *"What do I want"?* well, that is easy to answer' again he coughed, this time bringing up the gunk, from deep in his chest. He hawked the gobbet, onto the concrete floor 'I want what belongs to me'

'YOU'! he should have known '**Your the one who's been emailing me, with those threats**"!

'Coorrrect'!

'So'? Monty had started to calm down 'What is it that I have, that you could possibly want'?

'That's better'

'So, are you going to tell me, or are you going to keep playing silly games'?

'Trust me, I'm not playing games. I can see your point, though'

'Yiphee' Monty grumbled sarcastically.

The shadow shrouded stranger, suddenly showed a pique of anger '**This isn't a game. You need to realise, just how much danger you're in**'!

'Are you threatening me'? he wished he felt as strong as he sounded.

'**I don't make threats**'! his voice was harsh '**I just give you a warning. If you don't comply, then that's your problem**'!

'But I've done nothing wrong, so why would you want to hurt me'?

'It's not a case of right, or wrong. It's just the way it is'

'But that's not fair' Monty was ashamed of the winging tone in his voice.

'That's the trouble with life, it never runs the way that

you want it to' the stranger watched, as Monty fidgeted, trying to release himself, from his bonds. He smiled, because he knew, that his prisoner would never get free 'Why don't I put you out of your misery'?

'Yes. Why don't you'!

'Hidden, in what is now your home, is something that I've been searching for, for many years'

'How come you think that, I will find what you can't'?

'Because I haven't been able to look for it. For one reason or another, whenever I tried to get into the fort, something happened to stop me, so I never got the chance to have a look around'

'Like me, moving in'

'Exactly'

'All you had to do, was ask me if you wanted to have a look at my place'

'There's only one problem, with that suggestion'

'Oh and what's that'?

'I would have to reveal myself, and I can't afford to do that'

'Why not'?

'That's not important. What *is,* important, is that you understand just what is at risk here. Not only is *your* life in danger, but so are thousands, If not millions, of others'

'But' : - Monty's question was cut off, before it could be asked.

'Don't keep interrupting me, and you may well learn something' he waited, but his prisoner kept quiet 'What I'm looking for, is either a set of diaries, or, manuscripts. Leather bound and wrapped in oil cloth'

'How do you know that they are here. I mean, in the fort'?

'I've spent nearly sixty years searching for them, the last

place I looked, gave me a clue that led me to the fort'
'Where should I look'?
'My first guess, would be down in the magazines'
'And what do I do with them, when and *if*, I find them'?
'Keep them safe, and wait until I contact you' walking around the perimeter wall, of the derelict building, the stranger made his way, to the spot where Monty had been tied to an old chair 'I'm going to release you now, but I want you to stay here for ten minutes, before leaving. If you try to follow me, or see what I look like, I will kill you. It's nothing personal, that's just the way it is'

While Monty sat in his rickety old chair, the smell of the building started to registers on his senses. The odour of mould and stale urine, assaulted his nostrils. There was something else in the mixture of aromas. His mind searched for what it might be. Several minutes passed before it dawned on him, just what the smell was, that had been alluding him. It was the smell of death, that was making the hairs stand up on the back of his neck. Something, probably an animal, hopefully an animal, had died here and was know rotting away, into oblivion.

'Remember what I said, about not trying to find out who I am'! the voice close to Monty's right ear, made him jump, and as he flinched, his bonds loosened.

The only thing he knew about his captor, was that he sounded old, smoked and had bad breath. While Monty sat, waiting for the seconds to pass by, his brain became a whirl of questions. Should he involve the Police? Should he leave the Police out of it? Should he run? Should he stay? Should he ignore what had happened, as if it had never actually happened? Finally, with his mind screaming at him, Monty put on the mental brakes, forcing his beleaguered brain into a state of semi calm.

He decided, that the first thing he needed to do, was get home and get out of the clothes, he was warring. The smell of the place, in which he had been held prisoner, had started to seep through his skin and was making him feel sick. Gingerly, Monty stood up, pleased at least, that the room hadn't started to spin. Looking around him, he noticed that there was a slightly lighter patch of light, nothing more than a slab of very dark grey, within the shroud of blackness, over to his right. Nervously, and with great caution, he made his way towards the grey, and as he shuffled forwards, afraid to take normal steps, in case he tripped over and fell, into heavens knows what, he strained his eyes, trying to see through the stygian darkness. Finally, as his hand passed into and then through, the darkness, he realised that this was a doorway. Leaning against the wall, at the left hand side of the opening, he carefully took a peek through the hole, as if he expected his tormentor to be waiting on the other side, ready to attack him. All that met his searching eyes, was more intense darkness. Looking to the right, his heart leapt for joy when he saw the faint shimmer of sunlight. Monty realised that he was in some sort of corridor, because the sounds of his footsteps, where echoing back from the walls. As he walked, closing the gap between himself and the light, Monty recited a silent prayer.
'Please help me be safe. Let me get home'
On and on he whispered, until the words became a litany. Turning left and then right, he finally walked out, into blinding sunlight. The fresh salty air, never smelt so good, or the sunlight on his face, so welcome. The gentle

lapping of the wavelets, acting as a balm to sooth frayed nerves. Closing his eyes he turned his face sky wards, breathing in deeply through his nose and out through his mouth. The fresh clean air driving out most of the staleness, that had clawed its way into his lungs, when he had been held captive inside.

'Thank you' his sentiment was heart felt and sincere, as he thanked God for his deliverance 'Thank you' he said again, just for good measure.

Chapter Thirty

As Monty approached the massive fort gates, Duke came trotting out to meet him.

'Where on earth have you been'? the Site Manager, asked good naturedly 'We've been looking all over for you' concern shaded his face, when he saw the unease in his bosses eyes 'Are you ok'?

'Yes'! Monty stopped and stood looking at his Site Manager 'Duke'?

'Yes'?

'Err' he grimaced 'Nothing' looking wistfully through the gates, he said 'I've been for a walk'

'Must have been a bugger of a walk. You look like shi' :-

'Yes, thank you Duke'

Monty tried to walk past him, but Duke moved sideways, so he could block his path.

'We need talk'

'Not now'

'Monty, I don't wish to be awkward, but you're paying me to manage this project, and that's what I intend to do, even if it means that I'm being a pain'!

'Ok Duke' he relented. After all, what had happened, wasn't anything to do with him 'What do you need, to talk to me about'?

Monty's eyes were never still. All the time they were searching to see, if he was being watched. Some of his unease, rubbed off on his Site Manager, causing him to glance round, before talking to his employer, about what he wanted to do next.

'Some of the lads, have gone as far as they can. For the moment, and so, I'm going to move them on to something else'

'Hmm'? Monty mumbled absentmindedly, still searching for his invisible antagonist.

'And I know you want to use one of the old magazines, as a wine cellar and the rest for storage. So I thought, I could get them to have a clear out and'; - Duke jumped, when the other man threw a fit.

'**NO**'! he shouted, his face crimson with rage, or fear. Duke had no way of knowing, or telling 'NO! You keep out of there, until *I,* say so'! his eyes shone with an inner light, giving him a manic air 'You keep everybody out of there, until I've finished' he caught himself 'Until I say so'!

'What's going on'? Duke was starting to become irritated with Monty's attitude, he wasn't used to being shouted at, and he refused to be bullied by anybody.

'**Is that clear**'! there was a determination in his voice, that the other man couldn't help but notice.

'YES. PERFECTLY'! his voice had taken on an edge, and as he turned away, Monty touched his arm. Turning back, to look at him, he was disturbed to see the fear and defeat that nestled within the other mans eyes.

'Duke, I'm sorry' with drooping shoulders, his whole body seemed to have shrunk in on itself.

'What's going on'? again he asked the question, but this time, his voice was quieter, reflecting his concern.

'I can't tell you'

'You *can* trust me, you know'

'I don't doubt that for a minute' smiling unhappily, he took a deep almost sighing breath 'But if I tell you' again, he faltered 'if I tell you, then I may be putting you in danger as well'

'**Danger**'! his voice had risen slightly 'What could you have done, that could possibly cause anyone to be in danger'?

'I haven't done anything' : -

'But you just said' : -

Monty held up his hand to stop him 'I haven't done anything' even feeling as he did, Monty had to smile at the look of consternation on Duke's face 'It's what will happen, if I *don't,* do anything, that will cause trouble'

'Now you have lost me'

Monty took another nervous survey, of the surrounding trees and ditches 'Why don't we go inside, away from prying eyes'?

'Prying eyes'? Duke repeated. Monty's paranoia, was infectious and so he to, looked to see if anyone was watching them.

Chapter Thirty One

Monty stood looking out of his office window, and along the river towards the estuary, were the Thames emptied itself into the English Channel.

All his dreams, everything that he had done, every penny that he had saved, had been for this. His life long ambition, of owning and living in this old fort. And he'd be damned, if he would let it be spoilt, by some man, who hadn't even got the guts, to show his face.

Turning back to face into the room, he looked directly into the eyes of Duke, his Site Manager.

'What I'm going to tell you, is for you to know only. You must give me your word, that you will never tell another living soul'!

'But I don't' : -

'**Give me you word**'! Monty wasn't shouting, but his words held such gravity, that the man before him, felt almost pummelled by them.

'Ok, ok. You have my word'!

'Thank' : - Monty's sentence was cut off.

'As long as you're not into something illegal'?

'That's a difficult question to answer' Duke raised his eyebrows 'But I'll need you to give me your word again'

'You got it'

'You wanted to know where I've been' Monty pulled his chair, out from behind his desk and sat down 'Well, I *had*, been for a walk'

'Thought so' Duke smiled.

'But something happened'

'Oh'? his voice dipped, as he became even more interested.

'Yes' Monty grimaced *'Oh'!*

'So what happened'?

Monty told Duke all that had happened to him, since he had bccn gonc.

Duke whistled 'And you never saw this bloke'?

'No'

'Have you any idea, what this thing is, that this nut case wants'?

Monty rubbed the palms of his hands, on the thighs of his jeans 'No' he lied 'Well sort of'

'So, are you going to put me out of my misery, or not'?

'I'm supposed to have some sort of diary, or manuscript, hidden here'

'What, here'? Duke indicated the office, in which both men sat, with a flick of his right hand.

'No. Down in the magazines'

'It all makes sense now' he finally understood Monty's outburst, when he suggested, that some of the workmen start work on cleaning out the old ammunition stores

'This nutter, thinks that these diaries, or whatever, are down there, does he'?

'Seems that way' Monty was having severe doubts, about telling this man about what had gone on. If this all went horribly wrong, then this innocent man, could very well become a victim.

'Look, why don't I go and sort out the labourers, then I'll come and give you a hand'?

'That's very kind of you, but if the' what should he call him 'The' : -

'Looney'? Duke offered.

'I understand your sentiment, but this man is no *looney,*

believe me' an involuntary shiver, made him pull his fleece a bit tighter around himself 'Let's just call him. *Noname.* If Noname, finds out that you know about my *problem,* you could be in great danger'

'Maybe, maybe not. But you can't do this on your own'

'True'

'So, it looks like you're stuck with me'

'Ok then, but just as long, as you know the dangers involved'

'I do'

Both men nodded.

Duke went to do what he had to do, while Monty made his way down to the steel blast doors, that closed off and protected the magazines.

Touching the cold steel with his fingertips, Monty tried to imagine what it must have been like, down here, when the fort was first built, and on through the reign of Queen Victoria. Then the modernisations of the First and Second World War's. Slowly, he started to feel that he was suffocating, under the mounting weight of all that history. With a shudder, he realised that he was starting to imagine, that he could hear the scrape of metal on metal, as the heavy shells, for the main casement guns, were raised to the surface, and the shouts of the N. C. O's. as they barked out their orders. A slight breeze, which had somehow managed to find its way down to where he stood, through the maze of corridors and stairways, touched his cheek and he was glad, that he was holding a torch and not a candle, because he knew that the draught would have been to strong, for the flame, which would have been snuffed out, plunging him into a man eating darkness. With a shake, Monty roused himself, from the fanciful daydream, into which he had started to lose himself. Putting both hands on the cold metal surface, of the right hand blast door, he gave it a gentle push. Nothing happened. So he put his shoulder against the heavy panel and heaved with all his might. The door never even wobbled. Taking the torch out of his mouth, where he had placed it, so as to free up both hands, he stood back, so that he could survey the massive door. The reason that it wouldn't move, became instantly apparent. There was a large metal bar, that had been swung down and anchored, into an "L" shaped rest. This bar held both of the doors closed and unmovable in their current position. He had been so busy fantasizing about the past, that he hadn't really taken any notice, of how the doors worked. Assuming that all he would need to do, was just give them a bit of a push. Now, as he looked at the metal bar, he noticed how it was fixed in the middle, by a large bolt, which acted as a pivot point, and in theory, all he would have to do, would be to get hold of the left hand end, and push. This should cause the arm to rise up. Walking to the left, Monty again, placed the torch between his teeth. Placing his hands on the end of the flat iron bar, he pulled. As the bar passed his waist, he changed his grip, pushing instead. With a satisfying groan, the metal bar went all the way, until it clunked into its stops. The sound held a melancholy note, which echoed back off the solid walls, wrapping itself around him like a shroud. Giving the right hand door a shove, Monty smiled, as the heavy blast door swung open, on hinges that were amazingly, still well greased. There was a low rumble, as the door settled back against the wall. The rumble bounced around the granite block magazine, finally disappearing of into the distance, giving him some idea of just how large, the chamber, on whose threshold he now stood, actually was. Without stepping inside, Monty shone the beam of the torch, into the magazine. The darkness seemed to eat the halogen light. It was impossible to see the other side. When he moved the light up at the ceiling, his jaw gaped in awe, at the sight of the beautiful vaulting. Even though he had seen the upper parts of the fort, time hadn't allowed him to have a look at all of the rooms, below ground, so he'd had to trust the surveyors and architects reports and photographs. None of which, did justice to the majesty of this hidden treasure. The architecture, was simply stunning.

'Wow' Monty's mouth dropped open, as he looked around at all the work, that had been done by the stone masons.

'Fantastic, isn't it'!

Said a voice from behind him.

Monty, who had been totally lost in his own little world, hadn't heard the other mans approach, very nearly dived for cover, only just stopping himself at the last moment. Instead, he ducked his head, stepping hurriedly to one side. Turning as he went, so as to be able to see his attacker.

Duke burst into a round, of loud tearful laughter. The look on his employers face, not helping to calm him. It was very nearly two minutes before he could bring his mirth under control.

'You should' : - another batch of hysterical giggles escaped through his clamped teeth. Swallowing, he tried to carry on 'Y, y, you should s, s, see your face' he spoke quickly, not sure if he would be able to get the sentence said, before he was hit by another wave of sniggering. Tears rolled down his face, as he fought to control himself.

Monty said nothing. Just stood quietly, trying to calm his shattered nerves.

Slowly, it dawned on Duke, just why Monty had been so afraid and his enjoyment at the other mans expense, turned to concern.

'Monty'? his voice had lost its mirth, taking on a serious timber 'You thought I was the guy who attacked you, didn't you'? Monty simply nodded 'I'm sorry, if I'd have thought you would have been so upset by my silliness, I'd never have crept up on you'

'It's ok. There's been no harm done' Monty's smile was more from relief, than anything else.

'But even so'! his expression carried with it, a weight of sincerity.

'Please, let's just forget it'! Duke nodded 'Right, where do you think would be a good place to start'? the owner of the fort, stood looking around. The task that lay ahead of them, was more than a little daunting and he only had six days, to find the diaries, or manuscripts. Or what? *Die?* Who knew. He certainly had no intention of finding out what, if anything, might or might not happen, should he fail to come up with the goods.

'How many magazines are there'?

'Three in total'

'And are they all in as good nick, as this one'?

'I have no idea'

'What, you never looked'?

'No'! Monty shook his head.

'And you still bought the place'?

'Yep'

Duke shook his head, in disbelief 'Well, I suppose, we need to find somewhere that could be used, as a long term, safe, hiding place. Not to easy to find, somewhere that doesn't offer easy access and of course, it must be dry'

'That narrows it down nicely then' Monty had trouble masking his frustration.

'I would suggest' the Site Manager carried on, choosing to ignore his boss 'Somewhere, no higher than a person, could happily reach. Because, whoever hid these things, wouldn't want to draw attention to themselves, by carrying a ladder with them' looking around, he added 'And it's not exactly ideal conditions, for climbing around'

'Good thinking' Monty looked for somewhere to begin 'Why don't you start at that side, of the doors'? he pointed to the left 'And I'll start on this side'

'Your're the boss'

'And don't you, *ever,* forget it'! Monty said jovially.

'Oooh, get you' Duke retorted, in an over done camp voice.

It took them the rest of the day, to finish searching magazine number one. They had moved old bed frames, rotten and rotting wood, the odd loose brick and all shapes, weights and sizes of detritus. The one abiding memory, that both men were left with, was the beauty and the craftsmanship, lavished on an area that nobody, but the soldiers, were ever likely to see. That was until he had come along. One thing that both men had realised, was that, if they were going to carry out a thorough search, then they would need more than just the torches that they had been using.

'We're gonna need more light, if we're hoping to be able to do a better job tomorrow' Duke broke the silence after nearly three hours.

'Yeah, I agree. So where are we going to get a lighting rig from'?

'I can borrow a generator and a couple of twin floodlights. That should be enough, for now anyway'

'Good' Monty patted Duke on the back 'Are you still happy to help me'?

'You bet' Duke smiled cheekily 'I've always fancied myself, as a bit of a Detective'

'Hmm'

'What do you reckon is so important about these book things'?

'I have no idea, but whatever they contain, it's very important to someone'

'I hate to ask the question' Duke fidgeted uneasily.

'Go on' he felt ill at ease, although, he wasn't sure why.

'How do you know that, when you've given this bloke what he wants, he won't' Duke couldn't bring himself to finish his sentence.

'What, kill me'? Monty frowned 'I hadn't thought about that'

'So what are we going to do'?

'At this point in time' his shoulders rose and dropped, in a shrug 'I have no idea'

'Why don't you call that copper, the one who's doing the investigations into the murders'?

'And tell him what exactly. That I was tied up, in an old water tower, by a man whom I never saw, because he wanted to get hold of some old diaries'?

'*That*' Duke raised his eyebrows 'Is a rather *big,* over simplification'

'But you can see my point, can't you'?

'Begrudgingly'

Looking at his watch, Monty said 'I think that we've

done enough, for today'

'We sure have. So what time shall we start in the morning'?

'That's up to you' Monty had decided, it was best if Duke decided on the right time to start.

'Well, my lot get here at about, seven thirty. By the time I've checked to see what they're up to and allocated work to anybody, with nothing to do, I reckon I could be ready by nine'

'Ok' if I meet you at the store shed, we can bring the generator and lights down, together'

'Ok. Good idea'

Both men, took a last look around and left, to climb the stairs that would take them back to the surface.

Chapter Thirty Two

Monty and Duke stood by the generator, in magazine number two.

'I should have known, that it would be in the last place we looked' grumbled Monty.

'We haven't found the bloody things yet. So don't start counting your chickens'

'They have to be here'

'Why, what's to have stopped this woman, from moving them. And if this nutter is so sure that they're here, why hasn't he tried to find them before now'?

'I have no answer to your first question. But in reply to your second. He'd only just found out, that they were here, but before he could have a look, I' : - Monty smiled at Duke 'Me, you and your lot, turned up'

'Oh, how inconvenient for him' his voice was heavy with sarcasm.

'And me. Because the onus is now on me, to find these diaries, or face the consequences'

'We'd better get a move on then' the Site Manager muttered, as he bent down to take his side of the generator. Monty did the same, taking the other side. Both men shuffled into the corridor. With the load shared, they headed for the last of the magazines.

'Did you check your emails, last night'?

'No'

'Why not'?

'I knew what would be on it, and I have no answer for him, So I decided to ignore him'

'Ostrich and sand, comes to mind'
'Maybe. But I don't care'
'Tough talk' Duke glanced sideways at Monty.
'Not really, I'm just preparing myself to fight, if we don't find what I'm supposed to'
'I never had you down, as a fighter'
'I'm not. But when something's worth fighting for, like my life' he left the rest unsaid.
'Exactly'

After a little over two hours, of near silent searching, Monty made an announcement to Duke and the store room at large.
'I've had enough of this'! his voice held an angry growl
'There must be a more scientific way of finding the books hiding place'!
'like what'? Duke stood with his hands on his hips.
'Oh I don't know' he showed his frustration, by kicking at a brick, lying on the floor.
'Perhaps, we need to try and get into the woman's head'?
'You must be joking. The last time I tried that, I ended up in all sorts of trouble'! a smile touched the corner of his eyes.
'Yeah, but this time, the woman has been dead for years'
'So a nice easy option then'!
'Look' it was Duke's turn to show his frustration 'We've got to start somewhere'!
'Ok'
'So, let's think about the sort of hiding place, we, would look for. If we were a female scientist, with a couple of diaries to hide'
'Don't you think, that it's a bit late for that now'?
'It's never to late to change tac'

'But, if we didn't do this before, why bother now'?
'If nothing else, it'll break the boredom'
Monty laughed 'I'll agree with you there'
'How big do you reckon these diaries, or ledgers,are
then'?
'At a guess' Monty frowned, as he thought 'I can only
think, that they would be about' he held his hands apart
'Oh, I don't know. Twelve inches by ten'
'So, we're looking for a space, roughly the size of a shoe
box'?
'Yes, I suppose we are' Monty agreed.
'In that case, there's nowhere in here that fits the bill'
'But there has to be'! Monty almost shouted in
frustration 'This is where the guy, in the water tower,
told me they would be'!
'But I thought he said, the magazines'?
'He did'
'So, that could include the corridors, linking these store
rooms, as well as the shell hoists'?
'Yes, I suppose it could' Monty, had started to feel more
optimistic.
'Why don't we go and have a look at the shell hoists'?
'Ok' Monty followed Duke, into the corridor.
Outside, and built into one of the central supporting
walls, were the remains of the ammunition lifts. These
particular hoists, had been installed during the First
World War, but had been rendered useless, by Army
Engineers, shortly after the end of the Second World
War, when it had been decided, that this type of
installation had no value, or place, in modern warfare.
The original means, of getting powder and shells to the
old cannon, had been by block and tackle, but it had been
obvious, that this would be far to slow in the heat of

battle. So steam was employed. Now, all that remained, was the iron floor of the old lift, along with the skeletal iron work, of the shaft itself.

Shinning his torch up towards the surface, Duke could just make out the underside of the doors, that would have acted as protection, in the unlikely event of an explosion in the shaft, and of course, to keep out the elements.

'This is some feat of engineering' Duke's voice held a note of awe.

'The whole place is'

'You ain't wrong there' standing back, he shone his beam at the floor of the shaft, and as he looked, he realised, that the front was, in fact, a single plate of iron, held on by four bolts. Right in the middle of the metal sheet, was what looked like a trap door. Duke got down on his hands and knees, to enable him to get a closer look.

'What have you found'? Monty had difficulty, keeping the excitement out of his voice.

'I'm not sure' he ran his fingers over the rectangle of metal, that was hopefully going to be the way in, to a space below the hoist 'But if I'm right, then this' he stopped for a moment 'Bugger'

'What's wrong'?

'The latch has been broken off'!

'Can't we break the panel in, or unbolt the big panel'?

'We may have to' Duke took a large screwdriver, from his coat pocket. After placing the flat end of the blade, into the hole where the shaft of the handle had once been, he gave a twist. At first, nothing happened. But then, as he increased the pressure, there was a scraping noise, as the tongue of the latch started to lift. Finally, with a screech of protest, the latch came up all the way, and the door swung open slightly, just enough for him to get his fingers in, wrap them around the edge, and pull. Slowly, the door opened, the old corroded hinges, giving a low, miserable growl. Surprisingly, after all these years, the Site Manager found that it wasn't as hard going, as he thought it would have been. Suddenly, the door was open and Duke was aiming his torch beam, into the soot black interior. Cautiously, he put his head through the opening and took a look around. It was just as he had expected. What he was looking into, was simply a small chamber, just large enough for a man to get in, so that any servicing or repairs could be carried out, if needed.

'What can you see'? Monty called impatiently.

Duke pulled his head and right arm, back out of the chamber 'It's just a service pit'

'Oh'

'But it would be a perfect place, to hide something' he smiled, at the look of relief on the other man's face 'I wouldn't get your hopes up, to soon' shaking his head, Duke asked 'Would you go and check the other hoists, to see if the handles on them, are broken'?

Thirty seconds later, Monty was back.

'No. They're all intact'!

'Interesting' was all Duke said, as he went back for another look.

'Do you think that, the fact that this is the only one with a broken handle, is significant'?

'I don't know, but I'm hoping' Duke stretched 'That this' he squeezed a bit more, of his body, through the hole 'Is what, we are' pulling back, he extracted himself from the service chamber 'Looking for'!

Finally, Duke placed a bundle on the concrete floor, between them.

Monty squatted down, Looking at the oil skin wrapped package, that was caught in the twin beams of their torches.

'Do you think that this is them'? Monty nervously wiped his mouth, with the back of his left hand.

'Only one way to find out' Duke nodded at the parcel 'Will you do the honours, or shall I'?

'I will. But not here'!

'What'?

'We'll do it in my office'!

Chapter Thirty Three

'Go on then' urged Duke.

Both men had been standing, one on either side of the desk, staring down at the dirty bundle, that now sat forlornly, on Monty's blotter.

'I' his voice cracked 'I, don't know if I should'

'How are you going to know if these' Duke nodded at the bundle 'Are what we' he corrected himself 'You, are looking for'? he was almost willing, Monty to undo the string, holding the oil cloth wrapping.

Monty shrugged, before saying 'I dunno' he had just assumed that he would. Reaching out his hand hesitated over the top of the bundle 'Ok' he felt a sudden surge of paranoia, and so, in the hope of calming himself, he turned to the big picture window and closed the blinds.

'I take it, that you think we're being watched'?

'I don't know, but I'm not taking any chances'

'So go on then'!

'All right. All right'! Monty snapped 'I'm doing it. Ok'! reaching forward, he carefully took hold of the ends of the string. Gently, he pulled and nervously watched as the bow unravelled. Pulling the string free, he dropped it onto the table top. With a long sigh and then, a sharp intake of breath, almost as if he had felt a stab of pain, somewhere vital, Monty touched the oil cloth. Not quite sure what to expect, he left his hand in contact with the material.

'What are you waiting for, a bolt out of the blue'?

Monty glanced up at Duke '**SHUT UP**'!

'Charming' grumbled Duke.
'Sorry. it's just that' :-
'I know. I really do'
Monty nodded. Lifting both ends of the material apart, he lent forward and banged his head on the side of Duke's, who was moving in to have a closer look, as well. Both men looked up sharply, then burst into laughter. That seemed to break the tension. Opening the package, Monty lifted the two leather bound books, free of their enclosing outer covering.
'Funny'? Duke mumbled.
'What is'? he answered, not putting the books down, or taking his eyes from them.
'Those' Duke nodded at the books 'They may not be the biggest objects in the world, but they carry a weighty significance'
'You're not kiding'
'So you going to have a look, or what'?
'Suppose I'd better'
Placing both books down, Monty ran the fingers of his right hand over the grain, of the leather cover. Slowly, almost reverently, Monty opened the front cover and inside the first page, was the name, *Morrella Shlicke,* and the date, *1937.* On the next page, was engraved a picture of the German Eagle, below that, was the insignia of the, *Nazi SS.* What was inscribed on the following pages, meant nothing to either man, as it was in German. The next book, simply had, **1942**, written on the first page. However, it was the words that followed, that held the biggest shock. Even to their unscientific minds, the words made their blood run cold.

Chapter Thirty Four

Monty looked at the words on the first page, following the introduction. With a mixture of joy and trepidation, he notice that the scientific writings, were thankfully in English. In a shaky voice, he read out the terrible words.

'Aims of the project' he looked up at Duke 'To put it simply, we intend to repli' : - his voice cracked 'We intend to replicate a human being'

'Cloning'?

'By the look of it, yes'

'Surely, they couldn't have achieved it. I mean it wasn't possible, not until a couple of years ago'

'But if that's the case, why is Noname, so adamant that he gets these' Monty raised the book he was holding. Duke just shrugged 'The reason' Monty continued to read 'To replicate, then replace, important figures within the enemy highrarky'

'Wow. I can understand the reasons and the desperation, behind what they were trying to achieve, but we can only guess, at the ramifications, if they had achieved their goals'

'I don't think it's a case of, *if*, I think they managed, to get what they were after'

'Do you realise what you're saying'? Duke sat down, and resting his elbows on his knees, placed his head in his hands 'They could have Cloned anybody, they could still be replacing people' suddenly the enormity of what they had just been saying, became to much for him 'How do we know if the people in control, are not just somebody's puppet copies'? Duke was almost shouting.

'**STOP**'! it was Monty's turn to raise his voice '*If,* they were doing these things, then they wouldn't need these books, or manuals, or whatever you'd like to call them'!

'What, you think they need these books, so that they can carry on with their experiments'?

'No'! Monty didn't know how, or why, but he had the feeling that what he said, was correct 'I think that our friend Noname, wants our finds back, so that he can destroy them'

'We can do that for him' Duke offered.

'Unfortunately, I don't think that will be good enough for Noname'

'I've just had a thought' Duke frowned.

'Oh'?

'What's to stop him from taking the books, and then killing us'?

'I' Monty thought about what he was going to say 'As we said before, he won't, not after getting what he wants'

'How's he going to know, that we haven't copied them'?

'But why would we'?

'Lots of reasons'

'But we aren't going to' Monty looked searchingly at the other man.

'You know that, and I know that, but he doesn't'

'So, what do we do now then'? Monty was starting to fret.

'We need to think, see if we can come up with a way out of this mess'

After several minutes had passed, Monty spoke. Words that he knew were right, but he hoped that Duke wouldn't do, what he was going to suggest.

'Look'! a smile fleetingly crossed his face 'This is my problem, why don't you' : - Monty was interrupted by his employee.

'Not any longer it aint'! a grim smile settled on his features 'I've run away from to many things, in my life and I don't intend to run away from this'!

'You've certainly picked the wrong fight, to stand up and be counted'

'You can't always choose what happens'

'You can still pull out, if you want'!

'I don't want'! he just wished, he felt so sure 'So what do we do now'?

'I think it's time we contacted, Detective Sergeant Hector Farraday'

Chapter Thirty Five

'So'? Farraday said, into the mouthpiece 'What can I do for you, Mr. Barrington-Wright'? for a moment, he thought that the other man was calling him, to complain about something.

'I'm not sure'? there was a momentary pause 'That's not exactly true' Monty coughed nervously 'That is' why on earth was he beating around the bush?

'Look Mr. Barrington-Wright, why don't you just tell me, what's on your mind'? his time was precious, and he hadn't enough to spend, on winging members of the public.

'It's not easy' his fear was getting in the way 'I'm sorry if I'm being a bit vague, but I'm frightened. NO! Terrified. Would be more appropriate'

Farraday's interest had been piqued 'I see. And what exactly, is it, that you are terrified of'?

'I'm not quiet sure of how to tackle this'

'Just start at the beginning, and we'll see how we go'

'Ok' did he hear someone listening in, on their conversation, or was he just being paranoid again? He decided that paranoia, was the order of the day 'I had a visit from a man, who I call Noname'

Over the next twenty minutes, Monty explained exactly what had been happening. Only twice, did Farraday interrupt him, to ask a question.

'Right, and you say that you've got these diaries, in your possession right now'?

'Yes'

'I'm on my way'!

'Hallo. Hallo'? no answer, just an annoying buzz 'Shit'!

Just over thirty minutes later, Farraday was standing, looking at the fort gates.

Chapter Thirty Six

The small pedestrian door, in the right hand main entrance portal, opened and Monty stepped out, to greet Detective Sergeant Farraday.

'Hallo Sergeant' Monty held out his right hand.

'Hi' Farraday took his hand.

'Please come in'

The Policeman followed behind, as he was led up the wrought iron staircase and along the veranda, until they finally came to the steps, that would take them to his rooftop office. Standing back, Monty ushered Farraday up first 'after you'

Farraday nodded his thanks 'So, has anything else happened since we spoke'? he looked over his shoulder at Monty.

'Hasn't enough happened already'! he snapped, then relented 'Sorry'

'No need to apologize' placing a hand on the doorknob, he gave it a twist and walked in. Looking around, he gave a low whistle 'Nice' was all he said.

'Thank you'

After looking at the desk, he asked 'I take it that, you've got them hidden somewhere safe'?

Monty walked past the Detective 'Not exactly, no'

'I see'!

'I don't believe you do'!

'Why don't you explain then'?

'I put it in a place where I hoped he would find it, if he came looking, that is' opening the right hand draw, he picked up one of the leather bound books, placing it on the desk, quickly followed by the second 'Then at least, all this would be over' sitting down, he looked unhappily at the Policeman.

'I'm afraid that it doesn't quite work like that'

'What, because I called you'?

'Partly, and also because, I know that in a situation like this, anyone involved, is in danger of becoming a victim themselves'

'So what you're saying, is that I've got no way out'!

'You're not on your own' the Detective gave Monty a reassuring smile.

'That's a great comfort' Monty's voice was heavy with worry.

'I know that it's not much' : - his words were cut off, by an angry Monty.

'Unless you can guarantee my safety, your *"Not much"*, actually means, that you can offer me nothing'!

'Mr. Barrington-Wright'! this wasn't a situation of his making, and he didn't see why, he, should bear the brunt of this man's bad temper 'May I remind you, that this isn't a situation that I, or the Police in general, have caused' he took a second to calm himself 'We, I, will help you in any reasonable way, that we can, but we can only do so much'!

'**WHICH AMOUNTS TO NOTHING**'! he was almost shouting.

Standing up, Farraday said sternly 'Perhaps, we should Leave this for another day'?

'Please' Monty lowered his tone, trying to calm down 'Don't go'! he swallowed, causing his Adam's apple, to bob, giving an indication of his nervousness. When Farraday sat down, he spoke again 'You must understand

137

just how frightened I am, surely'?

'Yes I do, but I can only help you, if you help me'

'I realise that, and I'm sorry'

'Really, I do understand what you're going through'
Farraday offered.

'Do you'? there was a note of doubt, in his voice.

Farraday nodded 'Perhaps I'll tell you about it one day'

"No chance", his subconscious called to him.

'Ok' Monty lifted the books, towards the Detective, who took them and after placing one in his lap, opened the other.

Farraday frowned.

In answer to Farraday's reaction, Monty spoke 'One is in German, at least I assume that it's German, the other is in English' he watched, as the Policeman swapped the books over 'If what you read is true'

Farraday looked up sharply 'You think these are a hoax'?

'I have no idea, it's far beyond me. But as I say, if they're true, then God help us. Because what is written in there' he pointed in the general direction of the diaries 'Could. No! Will, change the world forever, if it were to happen'

'I believe, that it may already have happened'

Monty stood looking at the Policeman, as if he had just admitted to something horrendous. Which in some ways, he was 'What, you already know about this'?

'To a degree, yes'

Monty slowly sat down 'What do you know'? he didn't think that Farraday would tell him anything, but when he saw the thoughtful look on the Policeman's face, he felt a spark of hope.

'What I'm going to tell you now, is strictly confidential, *and*' he paused for effect 'If you breath a word to anybody, it may add to your problems and may even increase your chances of being murdered'!

'Why doesn't that surprise me'! Monty had started to recover his composure, well a bit, anyway.

'Do you still want me to go on'?

'Yes'

'And you understand fully, what could happen, *if,* I tell you what you want to know'?

'Yes' Monty nodded his head dumbly.

'Right' Farraday sat back in his chair, making himself more comfortable 'I have also met someone, who is searching for these' he taped the diaries, in his lap 'But he wants to destroy them, before they fall into the wrong hands'

'Will you give them to him'?

'I'm not sure yet'

'Why'?

'Because I don't know if I can trust him, or what his true interest in these diaries is. Or, come to that, I don't even know if they should be destroyed, let alone all the legal implications involved'

'Bit of a mine field, isn't it'?

'You can say that again'

Both men fell silent for a moment, each trapped in his own bleak nightmare.

'Did he say anything else'? Monty watched the Detective, as he turned his mind back, to their conversation.

'Who'? he wasn't being deliberately vague, he just hadn't put his brain back into gear yet.

'Your contact'! Monty was showing greater patience, than he actually felt.

'Yes, he certainly did' should he tell this man more, or should he simply take the diaries and leave. Finally, he

made up his mind 'The man I spoke to, was part of a
security unit, assigned to protect the project, that this
scientist was working on' he grimaced to himself
'Actually, they kidnapped her'!
'This gets better by the minute' Monty shook his head.
What on earth, had he landed himself in.
'Oh believe you me, you don't know the half of it' he
wasn't even sure, if *he,* believed what he'd learnt 'The
project that the English scientists, and later on, the
kidnapped scientists, were working on, was given the
title *"Ghosting"'*
'Ghosting'?
'Yep. I take it, that you understand the aims of the,
Project'?
'Only from the little bit that I read, in the front of that' he
pointed at the top journal, nestling in Farraday's lap.
'And that is'? Farraday wanted to get an idea, of just how
much the other man knew.
'Only, that they were trying to, I suppose the word would
be, Clone, certain, important people, so that they could
control the enemy'
'That's it, in a nutshell' Farraday looked hard at Monty 'I
believe, that the man who's been causing you grief, is
what remains of the Commando unit, that had been put
together, to protect the *Projects* interests'
'But that means, he must be nearly eighty'!
'Yes'
'Surely that's impossible. There's no way, that he could
have done what he did to me, not at his age'?
- 'Not unless'?
'He is a' Monty could not bring himself, to say the word.
'CLONE'! Farraday finished the other man's sentence.
'NOT POSSIBLE'! Monty sounded more confident, than

he truly felt 'Is it'? now his doubt, was starting to show through 'But if that *is,* the case, then who can we trust'?
'*That*, is a very good question, and a question that opens us up, to all sorts of nighmares'
'There is' Monty stopped, to clear his mind 'I suppose' he looked hopefully at the Detective 'Another way of looking at this'
'Oh and what's that'?
'They need those diaries' he unconsciously nodded at the books 'To help them complete their task, and without them, they can't do what they set out to do'
'In which case, it's important, that they don't get what they're after'
'I take it, that you're going to take the diaries, back to your bosses'? Monty thought that he would have been relieved to get shot of, Morrella Shlicke's work, but the paranoia he had been feeling, since this thing had started, and had only just managed to hold, beneath the thin veneer of calm, suddenly poked its head up, and he was starting to worry about whether he'd done the right thing, in involving the Police.
'No, I'm not sure that I am'
Monty raised his eyebrows questioningly 'Oh, and why's that'?
'I think' should he tell this man anything, after all, it wasn't as if he knew him 'I think that, at least one of my senior officers, is having pressure put on him, to close this case down' he sighed 'And he's leaning on me, to bury the case'
'What do you mean, "*Bury the case*"'?
'It can mean all sorts of things. But in this instance however, I have taken it to mean, that I'm to give the impression, that we, or at least I, am working on solving

the murders, but in fact, nothing will be happening. Then eventually, the case will be put on the *unsolved* shelf. After a respectable period of time, the evidence, will simply disappear'

'But that can't happen, surely. And anyway, isn't that sort of thing illegal'? Monty was incredulous.

'What you, and the wider public in general don't appreciate, is that, because of the threat of terrorist activity, this country is in a constant state of high alert' even for him, this explanation held fear and a sense of claustrophobia 'Not since the cold war, have the security agencies had such a free hand, in the running of this countries safety. This whole situation, is a gift to those within the Secret Services, that seek an inappropriate amount of power, for the Intelligence Community' Farraday loosened his tie 'We're fast approaching the point, where *they,* will be setting the boundaries, and, the security agendas. And before long, they'll be the ones running the whole damn country'!

'This doesn't sound to good' Monty had had no idea, of how bad things had become, and just how threatened, not only his, but everybody who lived in this country, how threatened their civil liberties were becoming.

'By virtue of what they do, they become paranoid and mistrusting. In fact, it becomes as natural as breathing'

'Second nature'

'Exactly. Would you want these people running the country'?

'No'

'Nor would I'

'And if they get hold of those' Monty nodded at the diaries 'And were able to carry on with the experiments, then they would be able, to place their people at the head of every institution, or business, or in every seat of power, in the country. Nightmare time'

'Exactly' grimaced the Detective.

'So, what do we do now'?

'You let your man know, that you have what he wants, and then we set a trap'

'I'm not so sure, that that, is such a good idea' Monty's expression, mirrored his inner fear.

'Hmm'? Farraday nodded 'Ok' standing up, he looked down at Monty 'Do you have a mobile phone'?

'Yes'

'Right, well don't use it'!

'Why'? Monty frowned.

'Because, without a doubt, they know your number. Go out and buy a new one, make sure that it's a pay as you go, one. I'll do the same, when we get a chance, we'll swop numbers'

'Ok' Monty nodded.

'I'll see you soon' he held out his hand, which Monty shook 'Thank you'

'What for'?

'Trusting me' that said, Farraday left, leaving Monty to his dark thoughts.

After a minute or so, Monty sat back in his chair, before clicking the arrow on his computer screen, over the email icon. He had mail. After reading the first fifteen, he finally came to the last one. When he opened up the email, all it said was, *"Have you got them"?* Monty simply typed "YES"! then sent his reply.

Chapter Thirty Seven

Monty sat waiting, staring, nervous of the expected answer. Nothing happened. When, after ten minutes there was still no reply, he stood up. With a last look at the flat screen monitor, he sighed, as he picked up his car keys.

Looking for Duke, he called to him, when he saw his head bobbing up and down, in a circle of workmen. 'Duke'! when his Site Manager didn't look up, he called louder '**Duke**'!

The Site Manager looked up and waved. Quickly, he finished giving the workmen their orders and went to join his boss.

'Monty' Duke smiled at his boss 'How's it going'?

'Not good'

'Oh, what's happened now'? he didn't like the look on Monty's face.

Monty stepped back into an alcove, in the thick granite wall 'Well, he's of the opinion that, even if I hand this guy back the diaries, the likelihood is, that he will kill me anyway'!

'You mean, that we're both in danger'?

'No! I mean that, *I'm,* in trouble. There's no way, that he could know about you, and that means your safe'

'That may be so, but as I told you, we're in this together'

'Not if it means, that helping me, gets you killed'

'I'm a big boy, I can look after myself'

'I'll make that your epitaph, shall I'? grumbled Monty,

good naturedly.

'Cheery little soul, ain't ya'!

'Look, I've got some things to do, so I'll see you shortly'

'Where're the diaries'?

'With our friendly Policeman'

'Is that wise'?

'I didn't have a choice' his voice was almost mournful.

'So what is he going to do with them'?

'I wish I knew' looking around, Monty added 'As I said. I've got things to do, so will you hold the fort'?

Even with the amount of pressure loaded upon them, both men still retained their sense of humour, and they burst into laughter.

'How does the old saying go'? he scratched his head 'If you can laugh, while all around you, people are losing their heads' Monty's voice was grim 'Then you obviously, have no idea what's truly going on' Monty chuckled 'Something like that, anyway' both men looked at each other 'Anyway' a long sigh, escaped him 'I'd better get moving'

'Just one more question' Duke stood with his hands, in his pockets.

'Go on'

'Do you think, he'll give them to his superiors'? adding under his breath 'Stupid question really'

'Not as stupid as you think'

'Why'? Duke had a bad feeling about this.

'You don't want to know'

'Wrong'

Monty looked at Duke. Deciding that he had no choice, but to tell him 'Sergeant Farraday, thinks that his boss, is being lent on, by somebody from the Security Services'

'What. You mean somebody like Noname'?

145

'Possibly'

'So what's he going to do'?

Monty shrugged 'I don't think, even he knows'

Chapter Thirty Eight

Arthur Hobleday, aka, Agent Arrow, lowered his powerful binoculars and ground his teeth. This wasn't good. If his suspicions were founded, then the man, whom he had just seen leaving the fort, was a Policeman. But what disturbed him more, was the thought, that the objects held in his hand, were the items that he sought.

Adding another name to his killing list, caused him not one iota of concern at all. What worried him however, was the complications, that having a Policeman, so close to the business end, could bring. There was one ray of hope, and that was his control of D. C. I. Trevor Hornby.

Looking around him, Hobleday checked to make sure, that he wasn't being watched. Slowly he retraced his steps, back to his car. Before he got in, he picked some grass from the leg of his trousers, before dropping it on the ground.

Hobleday grinned to himself, as a thought struck him. People, he thought, could be cut down, just as simply as a blade of grass.

Chapter Thirty Nine

Farraday sat looking at the books, that he'd put on the passenger seat beside him.

'What am I going to do with you'?

'Talking to yourself Hector'?

Farraday jumped. Looking out through the side window, at the owner of the voice, he tried to sound pleased, when he spoke.

'D. C. I. Hornby'

'How are you getting on, with suppressing the information from this case'?

Farraday opened the car door, making Hornby step back so as not to be injured. Standing up in front of his senior, Farraday looked him in the eyes.

'I'll get on with the investigation, *and,* believe me when I say, that any evidence I find, will definitely, *not,* be suppressed!

'**Now you listen to me**'! Hornby was almost shouting.

'**NO**'! Farraday smiled sarcastically 'Bye' turning, he walked away.

Hornby went bright red '**COME BACK**'! Farraday kept going. Walking up behind his junior, he grabbed his arm, spinning him around to face him 'I think you need to remember, *WHO*, exactly it is, that you are talking to. You also need to remember your place'!

With an angry growl, Farraday grabbed hold of the lapels of Hornby's coat. Forcing him backwards, he slammed him into one the brick walls, of the Police station. A whoosh, of air escaped from between the superior

Policeman's lips.

'Take your filthy hands off me'! Hornby's voice had become shrill.

Putting his face close to Hornby's, Farraday almost spat his words, at the other man 'Do you know the only reason, I don't batter seven shades of shit, out of you'? when no reply came, to his question, he pushed his boss against the wall again. The D. C. I. was terrified and he speedily shook his head 'Because that would put me in the same league as you' for the first time, Farraday looked around, to make sure that he wasn't being observed 'But be warned, you get in my way, or try to interfere with this investigation, in any way, and I *will,* come looking for you'!

Farraday's threat, hung in the air between the two men, like a veil.

'You don't understand' Hornby's tone, was wheedling 'You have no idea, who you are dealing with, and what they are prepared to do, to get what they want'!

'WRONG'! he let the older man go. A look of sheer contempt masked his features 'I have quite a good idea, of who your puppeteers are'!

'In that case' Hornby lowered his voice, glancing nervously around him, at the car park and beyond 'You should have some idea, of what they are capable of'!

'Go away'! was all Farraday could bring himself to say. Then, just before he turned to walk away, he looked back at his boss 'Do you really think, that these people will let you live, once they've got what they want'?

'Of course. They told me, that all they wanted, was' again, he looked around 'You know'? he waited for Farraday to respond, when he made no effort to help him, he carried on 'The parcel'? smiling hopefully, Hornby

149

tried to get some idea, of whether, or not, the other man, had found what all the parties involved, were looking for, some of them for decades.

The mask of contempt, darkening Farraday's features, now changed to one of pity 'You really are naive, aren't you'!

Hornby flushed red, his embarrassment painfully clear 'Please Hector, I have a family' when the other man, just simply walked away, he called to him, his voice little more than a loud whisper 'If you don't give them what they want, then you're as good as pulling the trigger'! his answer, was the slam of the entrance door, as Farraday entered the Police station.

Hornby stood looking at the steel framed, entrance door, for several seconds, before turning away to face the car park. As he took the first few steps, that would take him to his car, a glint of light caught his eye. Glancing left, in the general direction of the visual disturbance, he thought he saw a figure standing just inside the tree line. The barrier had been planted years ago, to hide the Police station and the Cadet training ground, from the gaze of unwanted prying eyes. Staring into the shadows, all he saw was the cool darkness, that hid the inner secrets, of the now dense woodland. Shaking his head at his jumpiness, Hornby got into his car and drove off.

Slowly, a khaki clad figure stood up. After putting the binoculars, which he had been using to observe Hornby and Farraday, back into the large pocket, on the left hand side of his jacket, the lonely figure stepped into the deeper gloom between the trees, and in seconds, disappeared, as if he had never truly existed.

Chapter Forty

D. C. I. Trevor Hornby, closed the front door quietly behind him.

'That you hun'? called Linda Hornby, from the kitchen.

'Yes' he tried to sound cheerful, but only just managed.

'You're early'! she called from the kitchen, a rose in one hand and a pair of secateurs in the other.

'You complaining'? he feigned grumpiness.

'No, of course not silly' she placed her arms around his neck, giving him a welcoming kiss.

As she stepped away, Hornby took a leaf, that had worked its way into her hair, and stood looking at it, as if it held some deep fascination for him.

'Kids back yet'? he enquired.

'No, not yet' Linda frowned 'They're over at their friend, Will's' looking closely at him, she asked 'Why'?

'No reason' stepping past her, he spoke over his shoulder 'I'll be in the study, if anybody wants me'

'Trev'? stopping, he turned to look at her 'Is everything ok'?

'Yeah. Bad day, that's all' he lied. Well, only half a lie. It had been a bad day.

'I'll bring you in a cup of tea, in a minute'

'Ok' he acknowledged, not really hearing her.

Sitting down in his leather chair, Hornby took his mobile phone from the breast pocket of his shirt, placing it on the blotter, which sat on the top of his desk. With a sigh, he took a piece of plain paper, from the right hand draw and placed it in from of him. Picking up a fountain pen, he started to write. Just over half an hour later, he signed his name at the bottom, folded the sheet of paper neatly, before placing it in an envelope, on which he gad simply written, *Linda*. That done, he sat back and stared at his mobile. Not moving, he sat that way until finally, it rang, just a little after two o'clock, the next morning.

'Yes'?

'Did you get the package'?

'No'!

The line went dead.

Finally, he went to bed. But sleep eluded him.

Chapter Forty One

Hornby looked at his watch, silently cursing.
Turning over onto his side, he lay watching Linda, sleep.
Finally, he lent over and kissed her on the cheek.
'I love you' he whispered. Smiling to himself, as his wife
mumbled something unintelligible.

Getting into the shower, Hornby turned it to cold
and flicked the dial to full.
'Huuh, huuh' if anything could wake him up, a freezing
blast of water would.

Taking his suite from its hanger, he padded with
it, down stairs to his study, where he dressed quickly,
finally putting his shoes on. Going back upstairs, he
checked on his children. Kissing each one in turn, he
went back down again. Standing with his hand on the
door handle, he looked back up the hall, letting the
peaceful atmosphere of his family home, calm his fraying
nerves. With a sad shake of his head, he opened the front
door and left the house.

Settling into the drivers seat, Hornby plugged in
his safety belt and with a last longing glance, back at his
house, inserted the ignition key. When he gave the key a
twist, nothing happened.
'Shit'! he grimaced 'This is all I need'
The last thing he saw, after trying to start the car again,
was a flash of bright light. The last thing he felt, was an
instant of terrible, excruciating pain.

Chapter Forty Two

Linda Hornby, was thrown out of bed by a massive explosion, which blew the front windows, back into the house, in a shower of glittering viciousness, which shredded everything in its path, as it scythed through the air. Luckily, for Linda, she had been protected by the bed, that just a few seconds before she had been snuggled up in. Even so, there was blood running down into her eyes, from a cut just above her hair line. She could also feel something sticky on the front of her nightdress. Slowly, very slowly, she stood up. The glass shards from the double glazing, although no longer flying through the air, like crystal shrapnel, was still almost as dangerous to her bare feet. Without a seconds thought for her own safety, she crunched her way through the debris, to find her children. So fearful for their lives was she, that nothing would stop her, not even the pain caused by the lacerations to the vulnerable soles of her feet. Some of the damage, would take many years of painful operations and skin grafts, to put right, the worst of her injuries. Even then, not everything would be put back, to the way it had been.

As Linda hobbled out through the the bedroom door, onto the landing, she heard two things. One filled her with an almost overpowering fear. While the other filled her with an all encompassing desire to fight. The sound that had initially stopped her, was the crackle of fire, the second was the screams of her children. Limping along the landing, on torn and bloodied feet, Linda met her children, who stood huddled, terrified, beside her daughter, Shannon's bedroom door. Both children ran to their mother, burying their fear filled faces into the material of her nighty. Reaching down, Linda took hold of Keenan, her two year old son, and lifted him into her arms.

'Shannon'? when her daughter gave no response, she gently but firmly, prized her little girl away from her, so that she could look into her eyes 'Shannon, we need to go down stairs, and out the back door' she let that sink in first, before continuing 'But first, I need you to go back into your room, and put your slippers on'!

'But mummy'! she glanced down into the stairwell 'We're on fire'!

'I know, sweety' she gave what she hoped, was a reassuring smile 'So I need you to be quick' when her daughter just stood looking at her, she simply said 'Shannon'? the little girl looked at her, with big frightened eyes 'Do you trust me'? Shannon nodded. just once and then turning, went into her bedroom. Thirty seconds later, she was back 'Good girl' Linda put a gentle hand on Shannon's head 'Follow me' cautiously, the children's mother walked to the top of the stairs.

'Mummy, your feet'! Shannon's tiny voice, cracked. Linda looked down, and for the first time, realised just how bad her injuries were. And for the first time, the true pain hit her in a wave so strong, that she was forced to lean against the wall, at the top of the stairs, in an attempt to stop her from collapsing. Shannon, gently laid a hand on her mothers arm, her eyes filling with tears. 'It's ok' she forced a smile 'It looks much worse than it is' standing up straight, tears rolling down he face, as the pain increased to an almost unbearable level, she took the first step on her journey down to the ground floor. 'Come on' she whispered, through gritted teeth 'Let's get this done, while there's still time'

From a safe shadow, just along the street from D. C. I. Hornby's now shattered home, the khaki clad figure, stood smiling. The result couldn't have been better. If this didn't serve as a warning, then nothing would.

In the distance, he heard the blaring of sirens and decided it was time to go. So, for the second time in the last few hours, he blended with, and then, disappeared into the shadows.

Chapter Forty Three

Farraday drove his car slowly along the street, in which D. C. I. Hornby and his family lived. Well, at least his family still lived there. Gazing in amazement at the houses, which stood on either side, he struggled to comprehend the amount of destruction, wrought on this quiet suburb. For scores of metres in each direction, windows had been broken, and the closer he drove towards his ex-bosses house, the worse it became. Until finally, he pulled up outside the now devastated family home. For nearly five minutes Farraday sat in his car, the engine still running, his mouth hanging open, as his shocked mind tried to cope with, and make sense of, what his eyes were seeing. The whole frontage of the Hornby home, was totally wrecked. All the windows had been blown in, as had the front door. Part of the roof was missing and virtually the whole front sagged, as if the very foundations had somehow, been stolen away. On top of all this, there were the black smoke stains, which were the finger prints of the now extinct fire.

Climbing out of his car, Farraday jumped when a voice beside him said, in a high pitched voice, which was just one indicator, of the stress that the owner felt.
'It's a bloody mess Hector'!
Turning round, Farraday looked into the pallid face, of uniformed Police Sergeant James Edgehill 'What the hell happened James'?
'Looks like a bomb'
'I know what it looks like, but what caused this'? he

pointed at the house. His mind still to numb, to properly comprehend, what he was seeing, or what Edgehill was saying.

'I mean, it was a bomb, in the D. C. I's car'

'But where *is,* his car'?

The uniformed Sergeant nodded in the direction of a large piece, of mangled and wrecked metal, that had been forced into, and around a tree, ten metres, or so, up the street 'That's all that's left'!

'Oh'! this sort of thing, was something that he had always associated, with news reports of other countries, not something that happened on his own doorstep 'Was he in it'? even after all that had happened, between him and his senior, he hoped that the man had somehow cheated his would be murderers.

'Inside'? Edgehill asked. Farraday nodded 'Yes' the uniformed Sergeants voice, was almost a whisper.

'Shit'!

'The Bomb Squad, said that he wouldn't have felt anything'

'They would say that' looking back at the shattered house. he grimaced 'What about the rest of the family'?

'Ok' taking off his helmet, Edgehill wiped his brow with the back of his hand 'But his misses, has got a pair of badly lacerated feet'

'How'd she get lacerated feet'?

'Walking on broken blass'

Farraday looked questioningly at the other Policeman, before finally shaking his head 'Never mind, I'm sure I'll understand later' nodding in the direction of the damaged house, he asked 'Is it safe to go in'?

'Depends on what you mean by *safe'* Edgehill's answer, was annoyingly oblique.

'**James**'! the Detectives frustration was all to evident
'**Can I go in or not**'?
'I'd advise you to go in the back way, as the front is not particularly stable'
'**Thank you**'!
Just as Farraday was about to place his hand on the Suffolk latch, the back gate opened, and he was able to look into the scowling face of D. C. Steve Lucas.
'Sarge'! his expression made him look old, beyond his years.
'Steve'! when the other man stood back, he went through the gate 'Thank you' stopping as he went past, Farraday enquired 'You ok Steve'?
'Yeah' he grimaced 'Just came as a bit of a shock, that's all'
Farraday nodded. He fully understood what his colleague meant 'How come you got her so quick'?
'I was out with some friends, not far from here, when the call came in'
'Good evening was it'?
'It was turning out to be'
'I'm sure she'll understand'
'I doubt it' he answered sulkily, not sure how Farraday knew that he'd been out with a woman.
'So, why don't you give me you initial report'?
'Sarge' Lucas took the lead 'Why don't we talk in the kitchen'?
'Good idea'

159

Chapter Forty Four

Sitting down at the kitchen table, D. C. Lucas took out his notebook, not that he needed it, it was just force of habit.

'Would you like to have a look around first'?

'No. Give me your report first'

'Ok Sarge' Lucas flipped his little book open, to the first page 'Mrs. Hornby said, that her husband came home, a little after 2pm and went straight to his study, to do some work' his voice was flat and emotionless, even though it was one of their own that had been murdered, he still had a job to do. This was what he had been trained for, after all 'She said, he had got up around 5am, and she thinks, he had a shower. Leaving the house around 6am' Lucas stopped for a moment, taking a deep breath, before continuing 'The next thing she remembers, is lying in the floor'

'Has she been badly hurt, only James said something about her feet being injured'?

'Yes' the young Detective slowly closed his little black book 'As, no doubt you saw, all the windows at the front of the house, were blown in. Along with the front door. To get her children, she had to walk over broken glass' Farraday winced 'And then, she had to walk down the stairs and out the back. The flying glass cut her head, but it is her feet, that are the real problem' Lucas glanced up at Farraday 'The Paramedics say, she'll be lucky to walk again'

'Are the kids ok'?

'Yeah. Just shocked and confussed'

Standing up, Farraday spoke 'Why don't we have a look around'?

'Ok. But you need to be very careful, the explosion not only caused structural damage, but it caused a fire, which has added to the problems'

'I just want to have a quick look in the rooms, at the front. It's the D. C. I's. study, that I'm really interested in' Lucas just nodded.

After a cursory look in the shattered rooms, at the front of the house, Lucas took Farraday, to their senior officers study.

'Sarge'?

'Yes'? he answered absentmindedly, as he started to have a look around.

'Do you think this is connected, with the other business'?

'I would have thought that, that, was a high probability, yes'

'So, that means that you and me, could be in danger'?

'Yes, and so could Mr. Barrington-Wright'

'Do you think, that we'll get a visit from the bomber'?

'I have no idea' Farraday was walking around the room, testing the draws of the filling cabinets, as he went. When he found that the metal draws, he was trying, were unlocked, he moved on to the next one. Logic telling him, that if the draw was unlocked, then there was nothing of any value hidden inside. Finally, he ended up at Hornby's desk 'I think that this incident, may just be a warning'

'But why Hornby, and not one of us'?

'My guess is, that he had been given a chore to do, but he failed'

'And a bomb in his car, was his punishment'? Lucas was

gob smacked.

'Yes' Farraday had tried all the draws, on the left hand side of the desk, then the middle draw. Now, trying the top draw, on the right, he gave it a gentle pull, grimacing when it opened 'did the bomb squad, say how big the bomb was'?

'They say about thirty pounds'

'A bit obsessive, if you ask me' his fingers were wrapping themselves around the handle of the middle draw, on the right. When he pulled, nothing happened 'Ah hah' he smiled to himself, as he took a penknife from his pocket. Pulling out the main blade, he inserted it into the small gap, between the draw top and the surround, slipping the blade towards the tongue of lock.

'HECTOR'! you can't do that'!

Too late. With a twist of the blade and a tug on the draw handle, the lock gave 'Who says I can't'! he winked at his companion 'Now, let me see what we have' taking the draw right out, he tipped the contents unceremoniously onto the desk top blotter.

Lucas stepped closer.

In just a few seconds, Farraday had sorted a small pile of objects and letters, to his right. All that was left, was a piece of paper with a number on it, and a small digital camera. Lifting up the camera, he tried to turn it on. However it appeared that the batteries were dead. So, he opened a little door in the side, and after a quick look, pulled out the memory card, slipping it into his pocket, before closing the side door again. Placing the camera on the pile to his right. Just as he picked up the piece of paper, so he could take a better look at the number, a voice from behind, boomed a question that demanded an answer.

'**What the bloody hell, do you think you're doing**'? both senior and junior Detectives, turned round to face their inquisitor. Lucas swallowed, while Farraday smiled warmly.

'Chief Constable Wilson' Farraday placed his hands behind his back, passing the piece of paper, that held the telephone number, to his left hand, before holding out his right, in front of Wilson 'How nice' : - he never got the chance to finish, not that he had expected to, it was just a smoke screen.

'**Cut the bullshit Farraday**'! the barrel chested Chief Constable growled as he watched the two Detectives, through narrowed eyes 'I'll ask you again. What are you doing'?

'This is a crime scene. We' Farrraday nodded at Lucas 'Are investigating the murder of D. C. I. Hornby'

'I'm touched' Wilson sneered 'We both know that you hated his guts, and were quite happy to physically abuse him'!

Farraday felt as if he had been slapped in the face, but he covered his feelings well 'Hmm' he smiled 'I was just trying to warn him, over the errors of his ways'

Wilson stepped forward, his hands clenching and unclenching 'I warned you once before, about over stepping the mark'!

'What went on between me and Hornby, was private'

'Not when he spoke to me about it, it wasn't'

Again Farraday smiled 'did he make an official complaint'?

'No. But' : -

It was his turn to interrupt 'In that case, subject closed'!

Lucas stood looking from one man to the other, his mouth hanging open.

'Not quite' rumbled the senior Policeman.

'If you don't mind, we've got work to do'?

'And so you may have, but this isn't it'

'What'?

Wilson smiled happily 'You and your chimp' he glared
for a second at Lucas 'Are being replaced by someone
from Internal Affairs' steeling himself, ready for the
angry storm of words, that he knew would come boiling
out of Farraday, he was thrown by the Detectives actual
response.

'Ok' looking at Lucas, he said 'Come on Steve'

Wilson had become suddenly suspicious. Stepping in
front of Farraday, he blocked his path 'What's going on'?
he had to resist the urge, to pick the D. S. up, in his
massive fists, and punch the angelic smile from his face.

'You've just told me, that the case has been taken over
by Internal Affairs. So there's no need for us to hang
around' his manner was calm and confident. He held the
trump card, and he knew it.

'I don't trust you'!

Farraday shrugged 'I can't help that sir' again he gave the
Chief Constable a winning smile 'But I can assure you,
that I'm only doing as I'm told'

'That's what worries me' stepping back, he allowed the
two Detectives to pass 'But remember' he waited until
both men had turned to face him 'I'll be watching you,
and if I get so much as a sniff, of something suspicious,
I'll have you *both,* back on the beat'

'Yes sir' Farraday pushed Lucas through the study
doorway.

When they were a reasonable way along the landing,
Lucas looked over his shoulder, to make sure that they
couldn't be over heard.

'What on earth is going on'? his voice was a whisper.
'Not here'
'Where then'? his question sounded bad tempered, but it was only the force of his enthusiasm.
'Why don't we meet in the car park, of the old fort'?
Lucas opened his mouth to say something, but Farraday put his right index finger, to his lips, to silence his question before it was voiced 'Do you remember those old war time sayings, about, *walls have ears,* and, *loose tongues cost lives'?*
'No' Lucas answered in a confused voice.
'Well perhaps now that I've told you, you can think about what they mean, while you're driving'!

Chapter Forty Five

Standing beside his car, while he waited for
Lucas to arrive, Farraday looked around at the grounds of
the fort, the river bank that lay in front, and the farm land
which spread its blanket of rich soil on two sides. For the
first time it hit him, just how lonely this spot was. He
supposed, that a person could be forgiven, if they thought
that they were in the middle of nowhere. Although,
reality was of course, very different. Just a couple of
minutes walk, up the gentle slope of the approach road,
would have you standing at the gates of St. Mary's
church, while just a bit further on, you would pass the
first of the houses that made up this small village. Even
so, since the fort had become a private residence,
nobody, or at least, very few people, came down this far.
Most people, so it would seem, were of the opinion that,
Monty Barring-Wright, would not want them on his land.
That view, although right in part, only affected the
immediate ground around the fort, which included the
private gardens. Monty for his part, as Farraday well
knew, was only to pleased to have people use the park
land, and once the building and landscaping work, to his
private residence had been finished, he was hoping to
extend it to include the more public areas.

This was of no concern to the D. S., what did
concern him however, was the obvious ability of this
Agent Arrow, to come and go as he pleased, and, the fact
that the surrounding countryside, only added to his
apparent capability, of becoming invisible. Suddenly, he

felt very vulnerable, and he decided that he should, under the circumstances, get back in his car. A fraction of a second later, just as he was retrieving his car keys, from his jacket pocket, he heard a car engine, then he saw the nose of Luca's car, as it crested the top rise, of the entrance road. With a last paranoid glance around, Farraday went to meet the D. C.

Chapter Forty Six

'I think' Farraday addressed himself to the other men in the room 'That we should review the situation, and then you' he nodded in the direction of Monty 'Should move back to your old house'
'But that's ridiculous'! Monty started to object.
'It'll only be until this is over, and once you've heard what we've got to say, I'm sure you'll agree'
'Don't count on it' Monty answered defiantly.
'Well, it's your call, but please listed to what I have to say first'
'Ok, shoot' Monty sat down behind his desk.
Farraday stood looking out of the large window, at the river 'This morning, my boss D. C. I. Hornby, was murdered'
'You're shitting me'! Monty's voice rang with his shock.
'No, unfortunately I'm not'
'How'?
'Someone packed his car, with so much explosives, that it turned it into iron filings'
'Wow' there was a respectful silence, which carried on for what seemed like hours. Finally, it was broken by Monty 'I take it, that you think that the man who tied me up, is resposible'?
'More than likely, yes'
'Ok. So what happens now'?
'I'm going to review the case first, because I'm the only one, who knows all the facts' he glanced over at Lucas 'And we all need to be up to speed' walking back to the

other side of the desk, he sat down beside his colleague.
'Before you start, I think I'd better go and get Duke, my
Site Manager'
'Why'?
'He was there when I found the diaries'
'**What**'! Farraday's anger flashed in his eyes '**How do
you know, that you can trust this man**'?
'I don't. But I needed help' lame but true.
'Ok, you'd better go and get him then'
Monty left.
'I don't believe this' Lucas shook his head 'How many
people know about this, *top secret,* operation'?
Farraday just shrugged.
Five minutes later, Monty was back with Duke.
'You all know each other'? he waited for the three men,
to nod their agreement 'Good. Saves on introductions'
after Duke had sat down on the floor, Monty regained his
seat.
Farraday didn't wait to be told, to go ahead, he just dived
in 'If I go over any old ground, I want you to listen
anyway, if only for the sake of clarification. I would also
ask you to save any questions until the end. Are we all in
agreement'? everybody nodded 'Good' looking around
him, he took a deep breath 'We all know about the
diaries. We also know what they contain. We are also
very aware that, the people who want them back, are only
to happy to commit murder, if that's what's needed to get
what they want. The victims, that we know about, are
testimony to that. And, with the car bomb that killed
D. C. I. Hornby this morning' there was a sharp intake of
breath, from Duke, which Farraday ignored 'We have
come to realise, that they aren't afraid to put themselves
into the spotlight' he looked at the faces of the men,

169

assembled in the room, and was pleased to note that he had their full, and undivided attention 'It's my belief, that Hornby, was being punished for some indiscretion, but I also believe, that the bomb that killed him, had another purpose'

'To act as a warning' Monty said quietly.

'Exactly' Farraday thought for a moment 'My contact' correcting himself, he then went on 'Our contact' he nodded at the other Policeman 'Has told us, that he will help in any way that he can. But this poses another problem. We don't know if we can trust him'

It was Lucas's turn to say something 'We've learned several things today' he glanced at D. S. Farraday 'Shall I'? the senior Detective, nodded his agreement 'D. C. I. Hornby, was in this up to his neck. It also looks as if Chief Constable Wilson, is part of the problem as well. Although we have no solid evidence, to implicate him'

'Yet' added Farraday 'It's my guess, and I'm sure that this comes as no surprise to anyone, that whom ever it is, who are after the diaries, and I can only assume that it's the Security Services, has managed to get their claws into the hierarchy of the Police force. Just how many people are in their pocket, and just who those people are, we have no way of knowing. Needless to say, I trust no one, except those that are here' what he didn't express, was his mistrust of the Site Manager, Duke. Not until he had proved himself. For the moment, he had no choice but to treat him, like the rest of their little gang. Even if he didn't tell him everything 'I must also inform you, that D. C. Lucas and I, have been taken *off,* the case'

'But why, and how do you expect to solve this, if you're no longer part of it'? Monty was incredulous. For the first time in days, he felt totally vulnerable and lost.

170

'To answer your first question. We're off the case, because Chief Constable Wilson, ordered us to hand the case over to someone else' Lucas answered.

'And to answer your second question. We may not be officially on the case, but unofficially, we intend to do our damnedest, to solve it' Farraday smiled at Lucas, who grinned back at him 'And in some ways, we're better off'

'How do you work that one out'? grumbled Duke.

'We have nobody looking over our shoulders' Farraday didn't quite believe what he was saying, but if it helped to calm some frayed nerves, who cared.

'But can you gain access to all the areas, that you need to'? Monty wasn't as easy to convince, as Farraday had hoped.

'Oh yes' smiling at Lucas, he looked at Duke and then Monty 'Not everyone is in the pay of the Security Services'

'Anyway' Lucas stood up 'I think that it's time, that we started to do our job'

'That's Steve's way of saying, that he thinks that I've been talking for to long' he chuckled 'But he's right. Sitting here, won't solve anything'

'Just one thing' Duke spoke quietly.

'Yes'? answered Farraday.

'Where are the diaries'?

'They're safe'! there was something about Duke, which put the D. S's. teeth on edge.

'I'd better get back' standing up, Duke nodded at Monty, then left.

'I take it, that you don't trust Duke'? Monty frowned at Farraday.

'It's nothing personal. I'm just not to sure, who to trust at

171

the moment'
Monty smiled. He knew exactly how the Detective felt
'So where are they then'?
'As I said. They're safe'! standing up, Farraday looked at
Lucas 'Come on, time to go'!
'Is that it then'?
'Yeah'
'So what do I do now'?
'You go home'
'But *this,* is my home' Monty was momentarily
confused.
'This place is to isolated to be safe'
'And after what happened to your boss, you think that I'd
be safe in suburbia'?
'Point taken'
'All I can do, is keep my eyes open, and my doors and
windows locked'
'That should do it' Lucas grinned 'Not'!
'Come on, let's go'
The three men shook hands, after which the Detectives
left.

Chapter Forty Seven

Since the death of her husband, Linda Hornby, had gone to live with her mother. Unable to face the reality of what had happened, she had resolutely refused, to go and look at what had once been the family home.

Now, sitting on the edge of the bed that had long ago been her's, when she was a child. She looked down at the envelope, held tightly in her hands. Just one single word was written in her husbands easy script. Gently, she ran her finger over her name, almost as if she hoped to gain some essence of her husbands spirit. All she felt, however, was a heart numbing loneliness, a deep sense of loss, that she knew she would never lose.

Slowly, tears started to find their way over her lower eyelids, then continued the short journey down her cheeks, until they dripped off the point of her chin.

With nervous fingers, she opened the envelope. Smiling, as she remembered how the young fireman had stood looking down at her, the letter in his hand, not quite sure of what to say, or do. Without a word, she had taken the envelope, forgetting about it until today. Three days after the explosion, that had killed her beloved Trevor.

For a moment, her sense of purpose deserted her, and she couldn't help but wonder, if her mother should be the one, to read the contents. Even in her turmoil, she came to realise the importance held within the words, and whether through intuition, or just a deep understanding of he husband, she knew that it was for her and her alone, to read the letter that had been addressed to her. Unfolding the pages, smiling when she saw her husbands neat handwriting, she saw that the words had been written, using a fountain pen. This fact, sent a chill through her, for she knew that Trevor only used this pen for important documents or letters, preferring to write them himself, rather that use a word processor. Cautiously, and with her mind steeling itself for any shock, she read on.

Chapter Forty Eight

To my ever loving Linda.

By now, I suspect that I have either been killed, or, I am in very great trouble. I need you to understand one or two things, before I carry on.

The first and most important, is this. You and the children mean everything to me, and I loved you all, with all my heart.

There have been three exceptionally proud times in my life. The first, was when we were married. The other two, were the births of our children. Please kiss them for me, and tell them that I love them.

You need to understand that, what I did, I did because I thought it was the right thing to do. It is only now though, I realised how foolish and naive I've been. Doing the "right thing", for ones country, isn't always the best, or, right thing, for ones fellow countrymen. One day, you may come to understand why I did the things, that have been asked of me. But for now, at least, all I can do, is ask that you trust me, and never stop loving me.

Some time ago, I was approached by a man, who asked me to undertake a project, that would help to ensure the security of our country. You will of course understand, that I felt I had no choice, even if I had wanted to object, which I didn't. How could I refuse to help protect the country that I loved so much? This unquestioning patriotism, blinded me to the truth about the people I am, was, dealing with. And, I came to realise, that this group of people, did not in fact have the blessing of our government, or, the Security Services. They belonged to what the American's call a "Black Group". This is a collection of people, sometimes within the same organisation, although more often than not, drawn from several like minded groups, across several Security Services. The members of this "Black Group", mistakenly believe, that they know what is best for their country. Better than the Government, and the various ministries. They try to influence what happens, by whatever means they deem necessary. Most have a warped sense of patriotism, but some are driven purely by greed. It is with great regret, that I have fallen in with the later. My attempts to extract myself from their grip, only meant that I drew out of them, threats against you and the children. Threats that I believed, and so I carried on, until finally, I failed. What has happened to me, is the net outcome.

I deliberately haven't told you the whole story, because to do so, would put you and the children at even greater risk. That is something that I would never deliberately do.

There is one thing I would ask of you. Would you please contact a man, who himself is in very great danger. This man, is someone whom I would not only entrust my life to, but also, those of you and our darling children. He is a man who has the rare qualities of honour, morality and an unshakable truth. If there is anybody who can stop this evil in its tracks, then it is Detective Sergeant Hector Farraday.

I need you to take something to Farraday for me. Something that I hope will help him, and go some way, to righting the wrong that I have helped to proliferate.

If you go into my shed, and make your way over to my workbench. Stand in front of it, with your back to the door. Look to

176

the left and towards the back of my bench, and you will see, that one of the planks is held down by four screws. Undo those screws so that you can lift the plank out. In the far end of the plank, you will find hidden, a data storage device. Take this to Farraday, and he'll do the rest. Under no circumstances, must you try to find out what is on the device. Because to do so, will put you in very grave danger. I beg you to leave it all to D. S. Farraday, to deal with the information, however he deems fit.

All that is left for me to ask, is that you forgive me and try to understand that, I truly believed in what I was doing, and that it was for the best. Also to say, that I will love you and the kids always, no matter where I am. I will also miss you dreadfully.

Your ever loving,
Trevor.

Chapter Forty Nine

Holding the letter to her heart, Linda wept.
Crippled by a deep pain of total loss, which settled over
her like a leaden shroud. She was confused about how
she truly felt, due to the mix of emotions raging through
her, not sure which one held the dominant position. One
minute she felt anger, while the next moment she was
consumed by loss, and then she was back to feeling
anger. Finally, she felt a heart tearing misery, mixed with
despair. How long she sat quietly crying, she had no idea,
but eventually, when she stopped, she looked around her,
seeing just how dark it had become.
'Just like my life' Linda said, falteringly, to the room.
Finally, Linda lay on the bed and fell into a deep,
exhausted and dreamless sleep.

Chapter Fifty

Linda sat looking at Detective Sergeant Farraday, who was sitting opposite, on her mothers floral sofa. With the kids and their grandmother out of the way, Linda had phoned the Police station asking for Farraday. When he eventually answered the phone, she asked him if he could come and see her. After he'd said yes, he had asked for directions. Finally Linda had hung up.

Less than an hour later, Farraday was knocking on the front door, of Linda's childhood home.

'How can I help you'? Farraday felt very uneasy.

'Did you like my husband'? it was an unfair question, and she could see how awkward it made the man opposite her, feel, but she didn't care.

'I' he thought about trying to make his answer more palatable, but decided against it. So he simply said 'No'

'Why'? Linda watched Farraday closely. Suddenly it was more about, whether, he told her the truth, than if he liked and respected her husband.

'I don't think that it's important, not now'!

'I do. So answer the question'? her voice was hard. Much harder than she meant it to be.

'Ok' Farraday settled back into the sofa 'If you want to know how I feel' he stopped for a moment 'Felt. About your husband, I'll tell you' suddenly and surprisingly, he felt more comfortable, than he had since he had arrived. It was almost as if he was being tested. A test that he knew that he would pass 'I haven't' he corrected himself 'Hadn't, known your husband for long. But when I first

met him, I thought that he was ok'
'I take it that you changed your mind'?
'Yes'
'Why'
'That's not an easy question to answer. In some ways, I
suppose he changed and became a kind of lapdog'
glancing at Linda, he grimaced 'I'm sorry if I've
offended you'
'It's ok. I need you to be honest'
'He started to bug me. Looked over my shoulder the
whole time, and he even rifled through my draws. There
were even veiled threats. In the end, I ended up despising
him' smiling gently, Farraday apologised again 'Sorry'
'It's ok' Linda felt a massive wave of resentment, and it
was hard not to focus it on the man in front of her, but
she knew that this situation, had nothing to do with him
'As I said, I need you to be honest' taking the letter from
her blouse pocket, she handed it to the Detective 'You
need to read this'!
Unfolding the page, he read the first few lines 'I don't
think, that I should be reading this. It seems to be of a
personal nature' he tried to give the pages back to Linda,
but she pushed his hand away.
'You need to read it' she repeated. When he hesitated,
she urged him on 'Please'
'Ok' he started to read the rest of the letter. When he had
finished, he folded the paper and gave it back to Linda.
Sitting, looking at the floor, as a whorl of thoughts raced
through his brain, Farraday finally looked up at the
woman before him 'Looks like I underestimated your
husband, Mrs. Hornby'
'Linda, please'
'Linda' Farraday smiled.

'Yes you did'!

The Detective flushed, with embarrassment 'So' he flashed a smile at her 'Did you find this, data thingy'?

'Yes' she held up a plastic encased, electronic device, about three inches long and about half an inch wide, with a key ring loop at one end, handing it to Farraday.

After turning the data storage device over in his hand, he asked 'What do I do with it'?

'You plug it into a computer'

'Oh'

'I take it, that you're a technophobe'?

The Detective chuckled 'You could say that'

'Why don't you get your young colleague, to do the honours for you'?

'I may well just do that'

There was an uncomfortable silence, that was finally broken by Farraday.

'I'm not sure why your husband chose me'!

'Didn't you read the letter properly'? she snapped. Her desire to be on her own so great, that her mood had become even darker, and she cared little, if she offended her guest.

'Yes' his voice was quiet and calm, he could understand Linda's abruptness. So he had taken no offence 'I did read the letter, but' how should he put, what he was going to say next? He chose the subtle route 'As I said earlier. Your husband and I, weren't the best of pals and our last meeting wasn't, shall I say, exactly friendly'

'Perhaps, it was because my husband was a better judge of people, than you are'! she looked away from the Detective, staring stoically through the window and into the back garden. Her eyes not seeing, her senses not reacting to any input, her heart broken into a million razor sharp pieces.

For the first time, Farraday saw just how much pain Linda was in. His heart going out to her 'Linda'? his voice was gentle and coaxing 'Linda'? he repeated her name. Slowly she turned to look at him, but without actually seeing him. Farraday was distressed, to see the emptiness in her eyes 'Linda'?

Suddenly, Linda came back into the room 'Detective Sergeant Farraday' it was almost, as if she had forgotten that he was there 'I'm sorry, I was' her voice broke off, as tears started to run freely down her cheeks.

Getting up from his seat, the Detective went and knelt in front of Linda. He took her hands, which had been working nervously in her lap, holding them gently, he spoke to her, his words showing only a little of his true feelings 'If you need anything, or if there's anything that I can do' : - his words were cut off.

'Can you bring my husband back'? Farraday slowly shook his head, looking deeply into her eyes 'Can you bring my children's daddy back. **Can you. CAN YOU**'? she pulled her hands, out of his reassuring grip.

'No' was all Farraday said. His voice little more that a whisper.

'Then you can do nothing for me' she looked at him, with tear filled eyes, which had already turned lifeless 'So, if you would leave' when the man didn't move, she added 'Now please'!

Farraday hesitated 'If you're sure you'll be ok, on your own'?

'I'm not on my own, I have my children and my mother'! as she looked at him, she saw the indecision in his eyes, realising that blaming him, wasn't the answer. So she smiled at him, and in a soft voice said 'It's ok, I'll be fine

and anyway, you must have work to do'
'If you're sure'? Farraday stood up, as Linda nodded
'Ok, but I meant what I said. If you need anything'!
'I will contact you. Thank you'
Quietly, Farraday closed the front door. Sometimes, he
really hated this job.

Chapter Fifty One

When Farraday had taken the piece of paper, with the phone number written on it, from the draw in D. C. I. Hornby's desk, he had known exactly who, he was going to go to, for help. There was no way that he could go through the usual channels, because he had no way of knowing, whom he could trust. "So" he thought to himself "The only person that I can trust, is a criminal". The irony of the situation, wasn't lost on him.

Getting out of his car, he slipped down the side path, of an almost derelict farm house. The farm land having long ago been sold off, for a new housing development, that had become known as the "Thames Corridor project". The broken slab walkway, took him to what had once been a well kept back garden, but which was now the same, as the neglected front. A tangled wilderness of weeds and briars. Working his way carefully around to the back, the Detective stood looking at the backdoor. Smiling as he regarded the hasp, that had been screwed to the door, he took it from the fact that the padlock was hanging open, that his prey was inside. With his foot, he pushed open the door, which surprisingly swung open without so much as a creak. Letting his eyes grow accustomed to the gloom, he stepped inside and immediately started to gag. He didn't know what the smell was, but what ever it was, had obviously died and started to rot. Slowly and with great caution, Farraday worked his way through the ground floor rooms, until he stood at the foot of the stairs.

Cautiously, Farraday looked up the stairwell and then froze, as he heard a click, close to his ear.

'I don't know who you are, but you had better have a bloody good reason for breaking into my house'!

'I hope that isn't what I think it is'!

'Oh, it's you' there was a mixture of relief and disappointment, in the mans voice.

Turning around, he looked at the man in front of him

'You didn't answer my question'

'That's because you didn't ask me one'

Farraday sighed 'Ok. Is that a gun, that you're holding'?

'I don't know what you're talking about'

Farraday held out his right hand 'Come on Frankie, give it to me'!

The other man smiled mischievously 'If that's what you want' he took the gun from behind his back, and held it up. Pointing it straight at Farraday's forehead 'Pity it's only a replica. Or I might have been tempted to end our long, and loving relashionship'

The Detective took the gun, checking it over, before putting it in his pocket.

'Oye. That cost me a packet'!

'You were robbed'

'Ha, ha' Frankie's laugh, carried no humour.

Farrday looked the other man up and down 'You really don't change, do you? You're still as scruffy, and' he sniffed 'And as smelly, as ever'

'Up yours. Who are you anyway, the personal hygiene Police'?

'If I was, you'd be doing a life stretch' Farraday looked at the floor, in the hope that he would be able to hide his grin.

'What is it you want'? Frankie pushed past the

185

Policeman, and started to plod upstairs.

'I need a favour'

'You've got some neck'

'Cut the bollocks Frankie. We both know, that you owe me more than I owe you'!

'And don't I know it'!

'Just shut up and listen' Frankie kept on taking the stairs, one at a time 'Where are we going'?

'To my' he thought for a moment 'Control room' he nodded to himself. Yes, he liked that.

'Ok, why don't we go, to your *control room,* quickly. Then we can talk'?

Frankie never answered, he just kept climbing.

Once through the door, Farraday stopped and stared in awe at his surroundings. The room that he had just entered, was in total and stark contrast, to the rest of the house. The *control room,* as Frankie had called it, was sparklingly clean and smelled of a mixture of polish and vanilla. Frankie, who had disappeared into a small side room, now returned. He also, showed a complete change, to the old Frankie that the Detective knew and despised.

Farraday stood staring at Frankie, who had not only brushed his hair, but had changed his clothes as well. There was also the distinctive smell of expensive after-shave.

'I'm impressed Frankie'

'Really' if he could have cared less, he would have.

'What's going on'?

'I'm getting my shit together' after picking an imaginary cotton, from his tee shirt, he asked 'So what is this favour you want'?

'I need you to check out a number for me'

'Why can't you go through your, *official channels*'?

Acting as if he wasn't bothered, he went and sat down in a swivel chair, by a roll top bureau.

'Because I can't'

'And what makes you think, that I'm interested in helping you'?

'I don't care if you're interested or not'!

'And if I *don't,* do what you want of me'? there was a nasty sneer on his face, that was really getting up Farradays nose.

In just two strides, the Detective was standing in front of Frankie. Grabbing hold of his tee shirt, in both hands, he lifted the man out of the swivel chair and threw him against the nearest wall, off which he bounced, landing in a heap on the floor. Farraday clenched his right hand into a fist, making as if he were going to lay into the scared man, who had scrabbled over to the wall and was now protecting his head, with his arms.

'OK. OK. You've made you're point. I'll do it'!

Farraday helped Frankie to his feet 'Right. Now that we understand each other, I want to find out who this number belongs to' the Detective handed him the piece of paper, that he had found in D. C. I. Hornby's desk.

'It'll take some time' he was hoping that the other man would go away, and come back later.

'It's ok, I'll wait' he was used to Frankie's delaying tactics.

Pushing the roll top, of the bureau, all the way back, Frankie pulled a laptop computer towards him. Lifting the lid, he turned it on. After a few moments, he taped in a password.

'I'm just going into the mobile phone directories now' looking back at the Detective, he asked 'Do you have any idea who it is, that this number belongs to'?

'No'! not exactly a lie but then, not the truth either.
As Farraday watched, row upon row of numbers rolled
down the screen. After several minutes the words, *No
Match,* flashed onto the screen.
'Hmm. Let's try a different directory' Frankie was simply
talking out loud.
'What are you doing now'?
'Huh'? he hadn't realised that he had been talking
audibly 'I'm checking the Government telephone
directories'
'You can do that'?
'I can' he answered with pride.
'Where did you learn to do that'?
'Now, that would be telling' for the first time since
Farraday had arrived, he was actually starting to enjoy
himself.
Suddenly, a red warning flashed up on the screen.
Farraday read it out loud "THIS IS AN *ULTRA HIGH*
CLASSIFICATION AREA. NO UNAUTHORISED
ACCESS". He didn't like this, not one bit 'Can you get
into there'?
'I suppose so. But I'm not sure that I want to'! this was
starting to get nasty.
'Why'?
'Because that is an area, that has a higher classification
than the Prime Ministers, mobile number'
'Are you serious'?
'Yes'
'Ok then, try and get in'!
'Is this gonna cause me a lot of grief, cos if it is' : -
'JUST DO IT FRANKIE'!
'Hey Farraday. I think you need to remember, who's
doing who, a favour here'!

'Yes you're right, I'm sorry. Will you *please,* see if you can get into that directory, for me'?

'That's better'! he saw Farraday's reflection, pulling faces at him, but he decided not to say anything.

'Any luck'? Farraday asked, after about thirty seconds.

'Patience man' Frankie coughed, to clear the nervousness, that had started to tighten his throat muscles 'These things take time' just then, the red alert disappeared off the screen, causing him to cheer 'Yeah. One up to the Frankie Man'!

'You in'?

'Sure am, and I'm checking the numbers as we speak'

'Good. Well done' he meant it to.

It wasn't long, before they got a result.

'That's strange' Frankie frowned.

'What is'? Farraday squinted over the other man's shoulder.

'Nothing really'

'But'?

'It's just that this number, belongs to a group allocated to the Security Services'

'Surprise, surprise' this wasn't exactly unexpected 'So what's the problem'?

'The number in question isn't tagged'

'What does that mean'?

'Well, all the mobile numbers that belong to the Security Services, are allocated, i. e. tagged. But the group that your number belongs to, has fallen into a black hole'

'Black hole'? Farraday echoed.

'Yeah' he gave the Detective an old fashioned look 'Which means, those that use these numbers, aren't on any lists, either'

'Black Ops'

'What'?

'Never mind' as Farraday watched the screen, he noticed a new icon flashing on the monitor 'What's that'? he pointed at the little flashing box.

Frankie turned back, to look at the screen 'OH SHIT'!

'What is it'?

'We're being tracked'

'How'?

'I must have triggered an alarm, when I broke in'

'So, what happens now'?

'I do this' he turned his mobile off. Then, after taking the back off, and the battery out, he removed the SIM card. Taking a pair of scissors, from a small draw, he cut the postage stamp sized piece of electronics, in half. Then he turned off the laptop.

'Why did you do that'?

'I can't take the risk, that there's some sort of bug in my phone'!

'What about the laptop'?

'The same' Frankie grimaced.

'I'm sorry. For the trouble I've caused you'

Frankie looked hard at Farraday, but could only see sincerity 'Right'

The Detective stood up 'Thanks again'

'What for. I didn't do anything'!

'You've done more than you know'!

'I take it, that we're even now'? Frankie looked hopefully at the other man.

'We are, at least until I want something' the Detective said sourly.

'You arsehole' grumbled Frankie.

Chapter Fifty Two

Frankie Spelman, was loading his backed up data, onto a new laptop, smirking as he stroked the keys with the fingertips of his left hand, and then lovingly caressed the flat screen. This particular model, was the top of the range, costing an absolute fortune. That was, cost someone else an absolute fortune, because the computer was nicked. Not that this fact worried Spelman.

As Frankie placed a CD into the optical drive, a noise from behind him, made him turn.
'Don't you think you've caused me enough trouble, for one day'? smiling, he strained to look at his visitor, his jaw dropping '**Who the bleeding hell are you**'? his eyes widening a fraction of a second, before a hole appeared in his forehead, and the back of his scull, followed by a mass of grey matter, exploded all over his new portable computer.
With a happy grin, the assassin unscrewed the lid from a two gallon can. Then, he poured petrol over the laptop and the stack of compact disks, piled on the bureau. Finally, the remaining accelarant was emptied over Frankies remains.

Standing in the doorway, the stranger took out a box of matches. Taking out a single match, he held the box in his left hand, placing the match between his left thumb and the striker pad. With his right index finger, held behind his thumb, the stranger released the index finger, flicking the match. As the taper rubbed against the rough pad, it ignited, and once released from his hold, flew across the room in an arc, flaring as it went. The match bounced off the floor boards, finally coming to rest in a pool of evaporating petrol.

The assassin stood watching, a satisfied grin on his face, as the flames expanded to engulf the still body of Frankie Spelman, then the bureau.

Farraday stood watching the backdoor, from what he hoped, was a safe distance. He had seen the stranger go in, and now he watched, as he exited the building and got into his car.

'Time I made a visit, to Mr. Barrington-Wright' Farraday spoke to himself. Turning to walk away, he didn't notice the smoke, that had started to escape the derelict house.

Chapter Fifty Three

'Hello Detective Sergeant Farraday' Monty had seen his car, as it had made its way down the slope, past St. Mary's church. So he went out to meet him.

'Hector, please'

'Ok. Hector. To what do I owe this pleasure'? the smile on his face was genuine and warm.

'I need to see your Site Manager'

'Oh' Monty frowned 'Can I ask why'?

'I just need to clear a few things up, that's all' his answer was deliberately uninformative.

'Ok, I'll go and get him' turning to walk away, Monty shouted over his 'Why don't you go and make yourself comfortable, in my office'? as he moved away, he noticed another car go past the church, and head down the slope. Looking back at Farraday, he said in a half joking, half serious voice 'You coming mob handed'?

'Something like that' the Detective answered humourlessly.

After a long look at the Policeman, Monty walked off, to get Duke.

'Hi Steve' Farraday welcomed Lucas, as he climbed out of his car.

'Yoe' when he'd locked his car, Lucas walked over to join the senior Detective 'I take it, that Duke is here'?

'Yeah' the D. S. walked off 'And we're going to have our little meeting in Monty's office'

Farraday was standing by the big window, while Lucas was perched on the edge of Monty's desk, when

Duke opened the door and walked into the room.

'Ah, Duke' Farraday smiled 'Please sit down'

The Site Manager did as he was ordered, and sat looking suspiciously from one Policeman to the other.

'Would you like me to leave'? Monty asked, unsure of what to do.

'No, I may need you to verify something' the senior Detective answered.

'Ok' Monty nodded, as he eased himself down, into his leather chair.

Farrday went and perched on a seat next to Duke 'Can you tell me, if you've been here all day'?

'Er, what, in this office'? his face held a secretive grin.

'NO' the Detective said patiently 'In and around the site, in general'?

'Yes'

Farraday looked at Monty 'Is that true. To the best of your knowledge'?

'Yes' the fort owner answered nervously 'Well, not exactly'

The senior Detective glanced at Duke, noticing how his eyes narrowed, as he looked at his boss.

'Can you clarify what you mean'?

'Well, I went looking for Duke, but I couldn't find him, and the others hadn't seen him for sometime, so I can only assume that he wasn't here'

'So, Mr. Ellington. Where were you, exactly'?

'Oh yeah, I remember now' he answered, not very convincingly 'I nipped out to the shops'

'And how long did that take'? Lucas spoke, for the first time.

'I dunno' he made a show, of pretending to think 'About forty minutes'

'And what time would this have been'? Farraday could almost smell the arrogance of the man, before him. There was also something else, but for the moment, at least, he couldn't put his finger on it.

'About eleven thirty'

'And so, you would have been back by about what, twelve thirty, or a quarter to one'?

'Spose so'

'**That's not right**'! Monty blurted out.

'Oh'? Farraday asked.

'No. I went to find you Duke, at about ten o'clock, and you were gone *then*'!

Duke sneered 'Ok, so I got the time wrong. I'm not a clock watcher'

'Why don't we start again, and this time you can tell us the truth'! Farraday's eyebrows rose up questioningly.

'Am I under arrest'? Duke's voice had taken on a surly note.

'No'

'Then in that case' Duke stood up 'I'm leaving'

'**Sit down**'! Lucas stood up, and stepping forward, he placed his hand in the middle of the other man's chest, giving him a shove

Duke stumbled backwards, sitting down heavily in the chair, he had just vacated '**Hey**'! he shouted '**You can't do that**'!

'Looks like he just did' Farraday looked at him, no facial expression giving away his feelings.

'Hector'? Monty spoke nervously 'Perhaps you shouldn't treat him like that' he swallowed 'After all, perhaps he did, just get his times wrong'

'Perhaps' Farraday smiled reassuringly at Monty, before turning his attention back to Duke, his expression changing to a mask of granite, when he saw the self assured look on the mans face 'So'? his voice was sharp 'Why don't you start, by getting your times right'?

'**Go to hell**'! Duke growled venomously.

Lucas stepped forward, slapping the man hard across the face. To the younger Policeman's surprise, Duke was up and out of the chair, in which he'd been forced to sit, and had grabbed him by the throat, attempting to squeeze the life out of him. Farraday jumped to his feet, taking the replica pistol from his pocket as he went, hitting the Site Manager just behind his left ear, with the butt end. Duke collapsed unconscious to the floor.

'You ok Steve'?

'Yeah' was the best he could achieve, as he massaged his damaged throat.

'Sure'? Farraday looked closely at him. The other Policeman just nodded, not wanting to use his injured larynx 'Good'! turning his attention to Monty, he almost laughed out loud, at the wide eyed, slacked jawed look of surprise on his face 'How about you'?

'Wha' : - was all he could mumble.

'Are you ok'?

Monty nodded dumbly 'Is, is, he dead'?

'No' Farraday smiled 'Just having his afternoon nap'

Lucas and Farraday, lifted Duke back onto the seat and then, used their handcuffs to secure him there.

'Some people have to pay, for this sort of thing' Farraday joked 'He' he nodded at the unconscious man 'Gets it for free'

'Urrh' groaned Duke, as he started to come around.

Farraday shook him roughly 'Wake up, sleeping beauty'

'What happened'?

'Let's just say, that an unstoppable object, met an

unmovable one. Net result, you got to take a short sleep'
'You hit me'?
'In a manner of speaking, yes'
Duke snatched his arm up, before he realised that he'd
been placed in shackles '**You can't do this. You have
no right**'!
'We're just restraining you, for your own good' Farraday
chuckled 'We can't have you harming yourself now, can
we'? he patted the mans cheek.
'**Barstard**'! he spat at the Detective.
'Oh dear, suffered from this is sort of thing long, have
you'?
'**Go s**' : - he never got a chance to finish, it was Lucas,
who hit him this time.
'**Detective Sergeant Farraday**'! Monty was aghast, at
what he had just witnessed 'Is there any need' : - Lucas
cut him off.
'If you think that we enjoy doing this, or that this is
normal practise, then you're wrong' he was shaking with
the effort of controlling his anger 'But this scum bag, has
just murdered one of our informants'?
Monty stared in disbelief, at his Site Manager 'What,
him'?
'Yes'
'Oh well done' hissed Farraday.
'I'm sorry, but he had to be told'
Farraday shook his head, before returning his attention
back to Duke 'So now *you* know, what we know'
'I have no idea, what you're wittering on about' Duke
smiled 'But you can be sure of one thing, when I get out
of here, I'll be straight on to the Commissioner. And,
when I've finished with you, they'll throw away the key'!
Farraday grinned 'That's if you leave here alive' for the

first time, there was uncertainty in the prisoners eyes 'If
you tell us what we want to know, then you may well just
get out of this, in one piece' the Policeman looked at the
bruises on the other mans face 'Battered and a bit worse
for wear, but none the less, alive'!

'What makes you think, that I know anything'?

'I've no doubt, that you're working for the people who
want professor Schlicke's diaries, but on which side, I
have no idea'

'What do you mean "Which side"'? Monty asked,
confused.

'Well, the way I read it, is that there are three different
groups, or factions, after the diaries, or logs, or whatever
you wish to call them'

'Shall I fill them in'? piped up Lucas.

'Why not'? answered Farraday, as he sat on the edge of
Monty's desk, watching Duke closely.

'Group one. They are not so much a group, as maybe one
or two people. What remains of the original guard and
the fixer'

Farraday saw nothing, in Duke's eyes.

'Our second group. This is of course, the Intelligence
Services. Although I have a problem with that one.
Because, even though there is a very definite threat, to
our countries security, they don't go around killing
people, and leaving the evidence for all and sundry to
find'

The senior Policeman was still studying their prisoner,
but still there was nothing.

'And so, that brings us to our last little gathering, of the
great and the good' he glanced at his colleague, who
nodded his agreement for Lucas to carry on 'The *Black
Group,* of which we know D. C. I. Hornby, was a

198

member. We also suspect, that our very own Chief Constable, Dean Wilson, is a member'

There it was. Farraday had seen the flicker, in Dukes eyes 'And I think, so is our guest here'

'Wow, you three really are clever' his insolence was still there, but he had started to lose some of his self-assuridness 'Except for one thing, you have no evidence'

'Not true'! replied Lucas 'Because our very own Detective Sergeant Farraday, saw you leaving the farm house, in which the remains of Frankie Spelman were found. After you'd shot him and then torched his place'

'Your word against mine'

'True, except that I have it on tape' Farraday smirked at him 'Amazing little things, these modern digital camcorders. Such clear pictures'

'Still proves nothing'

'Not exactly, but there's the thing' Farraday smiled broadly 'It doesn't matter, whether it proves anything, or even if it's admissible in a court of law, because you won't be **going**, to a court of law'!

'What do you mean'? a sudden dread, had settled over him, like a shroud.

'Well, one of two things are going to happen' Farraday stood up and wandered over to the window. Looking out, he had to fight the sudden urge to duck below the sill 'The first, and in my eyes, by far the best option, is that you tell us what we want to know. Then, once we've proven that your're not lying, we let you go. Or' he turned back, to face into the room 'I use you as a lamb, to catch a lion' he waited, so the words he had just spoken, could sink in 'You know, like they do in Africa, or is it India, if they've got a man eater on the loose' when Duke looked at him blankly, he sighed 'They tether a bloodied lamb, or goat, to a stake and then let the man eater come looking for an easy meal' Farraday saw the look of fear, on the other man's face 'So, to put it into our context. If you don't cooperate, I tie you up, then tell our Chief Constable where you are, then we wait. The only problem with this approach, is that your bosses will probably send in a crack team of specialists. While we of course' he nodded at Lucas 'Only being lowly Policemen, not trained for this sort of thing, may not be able to save you, and before you know where you are' his face wore a sad expression 'You're history'

'**You wouldn't**'? Duke swallowed.

'Oh yes we would' his voice took on a sing song tone.

'**You bastard. You dirty**' : - Lucas pushed a wad of toilet paper, into his mouth.

'There, that should quieten you down a bit' looking at Monty, he asked 'Why don't we go and have a cup of tea, while our friend here' he nodded his head, in Duke's general direction 'Thinks about the options, we've given him'?

Monty stood up and dumbly lead the way.

Chapter Fifty Four

'Are you really going to use him as bait'? Monty looked totally miserable.

'If we have to, then we will' Farraday smiled.

'I'm not happy with this' Monty was very nervous.

'You don't have to be' Lucas stood looking out at the view.

'But somebody could get hurt'

'You seem to forget, people have already been murdered' the senior Detective was starting to get annoyed, with their hosts whining.

'Yes, and if you have your way, then more people will probably die'

'"People", by that, I take it, you mean Duke'?

'Yes'

'Don't worry about him. If anything happens to him, it's just what he deserves'

'I don't want his blood spilt on my property'

'Don't worry, it won't be'

'Hector'? Farraday looked at his colleague 'I think it's time'

'Yeah' Farraday stood up 'Time to go and see, if the seeds we planted, have born fruit' he frowned 'If you see what I mean'?

Chapter Fifty Five

'So'? Farraday said, as he took the toilet paper, out of Duke's mouth 'Have you thought over, what we talked about'?

Duke spat bits of soggy paper, from his mouth 'I nearly choked'

'You should consider yourself lucky. At least it hadn't been used'

'Nice' grumbled Duke.

'Let's not waste any more time'

'Why not. Time, is something I have plenty of'?

'Not any more' Lucas spoke up.

'What's this'? Duke tried to act, as if he really couldn't care less 'Bad cop, bad cop'?

'**Shut up**'! Farraday sat down beside their prisoner 'It's make your mind up time'

Lifting his wrists up, as far as they would go, he asked 'Why don't you remove these, and then we can talk turkey'?

'I don't think so'

'In that case' : - he stopped talking, when Farraday took the replica gun from his pocket, laying it in his lap 'If you're trying to scare me, I can assure you, it's not working'

'Oh'? the senior Policeman smiled 'Then how come you're sweating so much'? Duke never spoke, he simply turned his eyes to the floor 'This should be a simple enough decision, for you' the Detective's voice had softened 'You either tell us what we want to know, or we use you as bait' after pausing for a second, he added 'The choice is entirely yours'

'I need more time'!

'You've had enough'!

The air in Monty's office, was filled with the static charge of anticipation, and, something else. Excitement.

Chapter Fifty Six

Farraday put his hands in his trousers pockets, as
he waited for Duke to make up his mind, on which
option he was going to take. As his right hand sunk
deeper, the tips of his fingers brushed against something
nestling at the bottom. Curling his digits around the
plastic, he pulled his hand out, holding up the data
storage device.
'Well, well' a smile brightened his sour expression 'I'd
forgotten about you'
The other men in the room, looked at him as if he'd
completely lost it.
'What is it'? Monty was the first to speak.
'It's a data storage thingy'
'I know that'! his voice showed his exasperation 'I
simply meant, it seems important to you'?
'Hmm, I think it could be' looking at Monty, he asked
'Do you know how to use this thing'?
'Yes'
'Well then' her handed it over 'You'd better show me
what's on it'
Monty plugged the device, into one of the USB ports, on
his computer. After a few moments of tapping on the
keys, he looked at Farraday.
'Looks like there are two folders'
'Really' the Detective,s voice, carried a sour note.
'One appears to be and audio file, and the other is a
photographic file'
'Can you get access to those files'?

'Surprisingly, yes'
'Why surprisingly'?
'Because, I take it, that these files are to do with the investigation'?
'Yes'
'So, something as important as this, would normally be encrypted, and password protected'
'Perhaps' said Farraday impatiently 'He wanted to make it easy for us, or someone else, to have a look'
'True'
'So'?
'Right' Monty looked from one man to the other 'Audio or visual'?
'Audio'!
'Ok' with a click of the mouse, the audio file was opened.

The first thing they heard, was a dialling tone. Then a voice,

'Hallo'?

'Trevor'?

'Yes. Is that you Dean'?

'I've told you before. Never use my name'!

'Oh, oh yes, sorry'

'Did you do what I asked'?

'Yes'

'And what happened'?

'We had to remove the problem'

At this point, Farraday asked Monty, to use the replay.
'Steve, do you recognise the voices'?
'Yeah. And that's without the confirmation of the names'
'This is all very nice. But what about me. Are you going to let me go'? Duke looked earnestly at the Detectives.

'**Shut up**'! growled Lucas.

'**Look**'! Duke started angrily.

'No' Farraday put his face close to the prisoners '*You look!* You're on very shaky ground. So if you want to stand any chance, of coming out of this in one piece, you'd better learn to do as you are told' he waited for Duke to say something. When he didn't, he added 'And you'd better think hard, about what I said, because make no mistakes, I will use you as bait if I have to'

'Up yours, you pathetic little arse' Duke hawked up a large gobbet of phlegm, spiting it at the Detective.

'**You'll be sorry you did that**'! Farraday spoke angrily '**You've just lost your chance, to disapear**'!

'Do you really think, that you can win'?

The senior Detective, simply pushed some fresh toilet paper into Duke's mouth.

'You didn't answer his question' Monty said in a mournful voice.

'Nothing is ever certain in life, except one thing'

'And that is'? enquired Monty.

'I for one, will fight to uphold the laws of this country, even if it means losing my own life'

Lucas smiled 'Very patriotic and rebel rousing'

'Did it work'? Farraday smiled. But even though he put on a relaxed front, he meant every word.

'No' chuckled Lucas.

Both men looked at Monty, then burst out laughing when they saw the expression on his face.

'Oh very funny' Monty said haughtily 'There's every chance, that we could *all*, end up murdered in our beds, and you two think that it's funny' nodding at his computer, he growled 'You finished with this, or not'?

Farraday and Lucas exchanged quick glances. Then the

senior Detective answered for both of them.

'No Monty, we haven't. So would you please start the voice file, off again'?

Without a word, Monty tapped a key, and the room again, echoed with the two voices. Most of the conversations were simply up dates, between D. C. I. Hornby and Chief Constable Wilson, but towards the end, the content changed, and the men in the room started to listen much more closely.

'Dean, it's Trevor' Hornby's voice carried an edge of fear to it.

'How many more times. Don't use my name'! *Wilson's anger was evident.*

Hornby just ignored him 'Something's not right'!

'What do you mean'?

'An innocent woman has been killed'

'That was unfortunate, but our man couldn't allow himself to be identified'

'Then you should have simply knocked her out, or something'

'Too risky'

'Then perhaps, he should have waited until the house was empty' Hornby's fear, had been replaced by cold anger.

'Not possible. We've got certain time restraints' Wilson's attitude was dismissive.

'I don't give a shit, about your time restraints' Hornby's heavy breathing, could be heard across the airwaves.

'Get a hold of yourself. You should also remember, who, you're talking to'!

'Now you listen to me'! *Hornby shouted down the phone.*

207

The line went dead.
*'**Son of a bitch**'! mumbled Hornby, as he re-dialled*
Wilson's number.
'Hello'?
*'**Don't you dare, hang up on me**'!*
'Oh, and why not. I haven't got time to listen to your
whining'
'This stops here'!
'No it doesn't'!
'Either you stop it, or I will'
There was a caustic laugh from Wilson 'And what makes
you think that, you, can do anything. You're just a
nobody'
'That may be so. But I do know, that if I talk to the right
people' : - an angry burst from Wilson, cut him off.
'Who's going to listen, to a washed up has-been like
you'?
'Trust me when I say, I'll take this to MI5, if I have to'
'You'll never make it' it was Wilson's turn, to feel fear.
'Oh, and who exactly, will stop me'? a kind of relief,
made Hornby's voice sound deeper. There was also
something else there, too. Confidence.
'Duke will'
Hornby laughed, before hanging up.

All three faces, turned to look at Duke.
'It was *you*, who murdered the D. I.'? Farraday grabbed
hold of Duke's head, wrenching it back, he grabbed the
ball of tissue paper from his mouth, with his free hand.
Tempted as he was, to push the wad down his throat, he
fought hard against the urge, the only reason for not
doing so, was that he had a use for him.
Duke smiled proudly 'Oh yeah, it was me alright. Good

bit of fireworks, don't you think. You should have been there, it was amazing'

That was the last thing he said, for some time. Farraday had smashed his fist into Duke's face, knocking his front teeth out. The blood from his torn gums, mixing with that, of his shattered nose. The Detective let go of the unconscious mans hair, and his head dropped, to rest on his chest, the free flowing blood staining the front of his shirt.

'Right' Farraday announced 'I've had enough of this' he looked at Lucas 'It's time to up the anti. You go and get us some of those weapons, you so lovingly hid away'

'What do you want'? Lucas had a smile on his face, that made him look like a little boy.

'Use your immagination'

'Ok' the younger Detective grinned, happy to be doing something at last.

'What do I do'? Monty asked nervously.

'You' Farraday looked at him, for a moment 'Can open up that second file'

As Monty flicked through the images, Farraday's smile broadened.

'Fantastic! We have all the evidence we need'!

'What are you going to do'?

'Start a little Black Operation, of our own'

Chapter Fifty Seven

Lucas drove his car along Love lane, whistling happily as he went. At no point since he had found the old Home Guard weapons store, and turned it into a private museum, did he ever think, that he'd have to actually use any of the weapons, he'd saved. As he pulled around a blind bend, he noticed a small, electric blue sports car, pulled into the side of the road. As he approached, a young woman opened the drivers door and stepped out. As she stood up, she pulled her skirt to a more respectable length, placing her handbag in front of her, almost as if it were a shield.

Lucas got a feeling of the young woman's vulnerability and decided that, perhaps he should stop and help her. Pulling over, he switched on his hazard lights, then got out of his car, to join the woman.

'Hi' he smiled reassuring, at the woman 'Have you got a problem'?

'I'm not sure' she blinked at him 'I think there's something wrong with my engine'

'Right. Can you release the bonnet catch, so that I can have a look'? he walked towards the front end of the car, looking at his watch as he went.

'Am I keeping you, from something important'? she flashed him a brilliant smile.

'Nothing that can't wait a couple of minutes'

After releasing the catch, as instructed, the young woman joined the Detective, who had lifted the bonnet and was staring into the engine compartment.

'I'm no mechanic, but I may be able to see something obvious' he tugged gently at the spark plug leads, checking to make sure that there were no loose wires. The young woman looked around, just to make sure that they were still alone, then, she put her right hand into the leather bag, still held in front of her. With a quick glance, up and down the road, she removed her hand from the main compartment. Flicking the safety catch off, she pointed the silenced automatic at the back of Lucas's head.

'I can't see anything obvious' he turned to look at her. With gentle precision, the female assassin pulled the trigger. From the moment the gun bucked in her hand, time slowed, almost to a stand still. This happened every time she was called upon to, *remove a target,* as her superiors quaintly called it.

She imagined that she could see the bullet, leaving the muzzle, watching as it spun slowly on its way to the target. Then she saw the lead slug, enter the back of the Detective's skull. She flinched when his face exploded, blood, bone and brains painting the cooling engine.

The nameless woman, turned to her right and saw two men, emerging from the bushes that lined the side of the road. They grabbed the body of the young Policeman, and bundled him into the boot of his car. Then, one of the men got in the drivers side, the other man settled into the passenger seat. With a squeal of rubber, Lucas's car sped off.

Time came crashing back into her world, and she ran to the drivers side of her little car, and jumped in. With a scream of the engine, she roared off in pursuit of her colleagues. A sly smile crept over her face and she

giggled.
'One down, three to go'

Chapter Fifty Eight

'Should't Lucas have phoned you by now'? Monty was getting itchy.

'Yeah' Farraday said, as he picked up his mobile phone, pressing the quick dial number, that would connect him to Lucas. All he got, was a recorded message 'Steve, it's Hector, call me'

'What's he up to'? Monty asked.

Farraday looked at his watch 'He should have been back, hours ago'

'Perhaps he's been delayed' Monty added hopefully.

'NO'! Farraday was certain about what he was going to say 'I'm afraid that he's been hit'

Monty sucked in a deep, shocked breath.

'Oh dear' Duke said sarcastically, through tattered lips 'And then there were two' he flinched, when Farraday stepped angrily towards him, bending down, so that their faces were almost level.

'And then there were, *three*, actually'

Duke tried to smile but grimaced, as pain shot through his gums and the area, around his shattered nose 'That's my lot out there, so I'm safe. But you and him' he nodded at Monty 'Stand no chance'

'Oh, believe me' the Detective spat the words from his mouth 'When I finish telling, "Your lot", about how you sang like a canary, they'll be baying for your blood' he stood up, turning away, so that their prisoner wouldn't see the doubt in his eyes.

'They won't believe you'

'If that's the thought that keeps you going, then you keep it'

'What are we going to do now'? Monty was starting to shake with nervousness.

'We put him somewhere safe. Then we go and do what Lucas, was trying to do'

'And what's that'?

'You heard what I said'?

'Yeah, but what did it mean'? Monty had been listening, but not hearing. There were to many things going round in his head. To many chaotic thoughts.

Farraday glanced at Duke 'I'll tell you later'

Monty stole a look, at his Site Manager 'Right' he nodded.

'So, let's get tossbag there' the Detective looked in the direction of the shackled man, and scowled 'Somewhere quiet'

'How are we going to get past the contractors'? Monty was starting to see flaws in the plan, already.

'We're not'

'Aye'?

'You're going to give them, the rest of the day off'

'Why. What will I tell them'?

'Nothing. You're the boss, remember'?

'Oh yeah'

Farraday looked up, at the vaulted ceiling.

'Wow'

'I know. It had that effect on me, the first time I came down here'

'Is this, where you found the diaries'?

'Just over there, in the base of the ammunition lift'

'What are you going to do with me'? Duke asked, in a

worried voice.

'You'll find out soon enough' Farraday answered, as he clamped the handcuffs, that were attached to Duke's left wrist, around one of the many pipes that cobwebed their way around the walls 'Come on, we've got things to do' the Detective lead the way out.

Chapter Fifty Nine

'What is this place'? Monty looked around him, his
mouth hanging open.
'It's an old Home Guard weapons store'
'What, from the Second World War'?
'The very same'
'Honest'?
'Yep' Farraday took one of the MK1 Lee Enfield rifles,
down from the wrack 'Do you know how, to use one of
these'? his voice carried a note of hope.
'Oh yeah, I go to work with one in my rucksack,
everyday' Monty shook his head.
'Funny man' the Detective lifted the bolt and pulled it
back, checking to see if it was loaded, both the chamber,
and the magazine were clear. Lifting the lid, on one of
the ammunition boxes, he took out enough rounds to fill
the magazine. Holding the weapon up to his shoulder, he
looked through the telescopic site.
'Do you really think, that you're going to need that'?
'Oh yes'
'We really are in danger, aren't we'?
'Finally, the penny drops' Farraday said absentmindedly,
as he looked around.
'What are our chances'?
'Of coming through this'?
'Yeah' Monty slowly nodded his head.
'Zero to none'
'That good aye'?
'What you have to understand, is that the people we're

216

up against, are professionals'
'So are you' simple but true.
Farraday smiled 'Thank you for the compliment. But
these people are, *true,* professionals' pulling open
another draw, he rubbed his hands together.
'So what does that mean'?
'What'?
'True professionals'?
'These guys are killers'
'I know that' Monty was starting to get frustrated, at
Farraday's lack of complete answers.
'**Look**'! Farraday took an automatic out of the open
draw, placing it on the workbench 'I don't have any, true
or accurate information, but my best guess is, that we're
up against the Intelligence Services'
'What, you mean, MI5'?
'Or MI6'
'How can we fight them'? he was starting to panic again
'Why can't we go to them, and give them what they
want'?
'If only that were possible'
'What's stopping us then'?
'You know why' Farraday spoke quietly.
'But if they get what they want' : -
'We're witnesses'
'So what'?
'Come on Monty, think'! when Monty said nothing, he
filled in the gaps for him 'They want us dead, because
they don't want anybody to know, what they've been up
to and the government, at least some of the hierarchy,
don't want the world to know, what they were prepared
to do, and are still willing to do, to get what they want'
'What you're saying, is that, whichever way we turn,

whatever we do, wherever we go, we're as good as dead'?

'Something like that'

'In that case' he held out his hand 'I'm going to take some of *them*, with me'

'Are you sure, that you want to do this'?

'Yes' he sounded more sure, than he felt.

'Ok' Farraday picked up the automatic, checked to make sure the safety catch was engaged. Then, slid in the magazine. Finally, he pushed back the block, to load a round of ammunition into the firing chamber. Holding out the gun, he invited Monty to take the weapon 'Here you go'? Monty took the gun, weighing it in his right hand 'Now remember, when you use that, if you have to, hold it like this' Farraday pretend to hold the gun in his right hand, with his left cupped underneath 'You aim, gently squeeze the trigger and then, aim again' he smiled grimly 'None of that Hollywood bollocks. If you fire off multiple rounds, you'll never hit anything. Are you ok with that'?

'Yes. I think so'

'Good' the Detective handed the other man, two full magazines.

'I take it, that you're expecting world war three to start sooner than later'? there was no humour in Monty's voice.

'Not exactly, but if we're to get through this, we're gonna need as much help as possible'

'Is there nobody else, that we can ask for help'?

'Nobody that I'm sure, we can trust'

'So we really, *are,* on our own then'! not a question. Monty was just stating the obvious, for his own clarification.

'Yeah' Farraday agreed, unhappily. Then, his face was covered by a devilish grin 'As you said. We'll take some of them with us'! taking the lid off a wooden box, he chuckled 'And have a bit of fun doing it'

Monty came and stood by his side, looking down into the box, that the Detective had just opened 'Hand-grenades'?

'Yes' he said, as he counted out about twenty.

'Where did Steve Lucas, get all this stuff from'?

'As I said. This was an old Home Guard weapons dump'

'I know. But why would he keep, all this ordinance'?

'He didn't keep everything, only some of it'

'Why, for what reason'?

Farraday shrugged 'Perhaps, he knew more than he let on'

'Or perhaps he was paranoid'

'Doesn't matter now. whatever his reason, the fact that he kept this stuff, has done us a favour'

'But this' Monty held up the automatic 'Is a modern weapon'?

Again, Farraday shrugged 'I know nothing' picking up two rucksacks, he placed two equal amounts of Grenades, into the large compartment of each 'Can you open that box, behind you'? he waited, while Monty used a crowbar to lever off the top 'And get me a dozen or so, out'?

'What are they'?

'Thunderflashes'

'What do you want me to do with them'?

'Put some in each rucksack' Farraday was opening and shutting draws, as he searched for the items he needed 'Aha' he said, as he opened a cupboard door. Taking out a shoe box, he took the lid off. The first thing he saw, was a cloth, and judging by the smell of oil, he decided that it must be another pistol. Lifting back the flaps of oil cloth, Farraday exposed another automatic 'This'll do for me' after loading it, he put it into his coat pocket.

Finally, he found the other item that he required.

'What do you want fishing line for'? Monty frowned at him.

'Trip wire'

'Of course, what else' he said, as if he knew exactly, what was going on.

'And you'll need these' he threw a bulky object at Monty.

Monty deftly caught the fast moving object 'What is it'?

'They' Farraday said 'Are Night Vision glasses'

'Right, of course they are'! it was Monty's turn to smile.

'Just a few more things, and then we can go'

'What are you looking for'? Monty couldn't understand what else, they might need.

Farraday looked long and hard, into Monty's eyes, before answering curtly 'Explosives, ball-bearings and containers'

'But': -

'I know' Farraday lowered his eyes 'Barbarick'

Monty nodded 'Yes' his voice was almost inaudible.

'But if I'm right, then we're going to need to take extra precautions'

Monty mutely nodded.

Chapter Sixty

Farraday and Monty, had moved Duke to the old gun emplacement, that nestled in a reedbed behind the modern sea wall, which stood approximately two hundred yards away, from the low tide mark.

They had placed him on an old mattress, before gagging him. Finally, they chained him to an iron loop, in one of the walls.

'What are we going to do next'? Monty asked, trying to keep the excitement from his voice.

Farraday nodded his head, at the exit, indicating that he wanted to talk outside. Stepping back into the shadows and pulling Monty after him, he spoke quietly.

'We set the traps. then we make the call'

It took them nearly five hours, to prepare their defences, but finally they were finished.

'Let's hope they do the trick'

'If they don't, we really, *are,* up shit creek, without an outboard motor'

'I couldn't have put it more eloquently, myself' Farraday slapped Monty on the back. Both men laughing, not with mirth but in the hope that, it might release some of the tension, which was knotting up their stomach muscles.

Farraday looked at his watch 'Two twenty seven' he confirmed 'Let's hope that they get here, before it gets light' taking out his mobile, he glanced at the other man, his uncertainty painfully obvious.

'Go ahead' Monty encouraged 'Make that call'

Farraday pressed the quick dial button, before putting the

mobile phone to his ear.

'Who is this'? the voice at the other end was angry.

'Hello Chief Constable Wilson'

'Is that you Farraday'?

'Sure is, fart face' he glanced at Monty, who smiled at him.

'What did you say'?

Farrday ignored the question 'I have your man Duke, with me'

'I don't know *who*, you are talking about'!

'Good try. But lets not waste your time and mine' pausing, Farraday took a deep, silent breath 'We both *know*, that Duke is working for you and your little group' : -

'**You listen to me, and you understand this**' : -

'**Shut up**'! Farraday cut him off.

'You're going to regret this'

'I have the diaries, and I have Duke. If you want them back, you'll have to come and get them'

'As I said. I don't know' :-

'Fine, have it your way. But I'm sure that the press will have a field day, when I show them what I have'

'**WAIT**'!!! Wilson nearly exploded.

'Why. I thought that you weren't interested'?

'Where are you'?

'The old fort'

'What, with that idiot Barrington-Wright'?

'No'

'Where then'?

'There's an old gun emplacement, in the fort grounds, near the river. Duke and the diaries are there'

'What do you want'? Wilson's voice was laced with suspicion.

'To be left alone, to do my job'
'After all that's happened, I don't think so'! Wilson almost laughed out loud.
Farraday hung up.
'Is he coming'? Monty asked expectantly.
'He may not come himself, but believe me, somebody will'
'What do we do now'? Monty looked around nervously.
'We take up our positions, and wait'

     Both men walked to a dip in the sea wall, about fifty yards away, where they had a good all-round view of the local area. Jumping into the hollow, Farraday waited until Monty had ducked down, before pulling the green tarpaulin over them.
'What now'? Monty's voice was shaky.
'We stay alert, and keep our eyes open'

They didn't have long to wait.

Chapter Sixty One

'Hector'? Monty glanced in Farraday's general direction, only his dim outline was visible to him.

'What'? he sighed.

'We've got company'

The Detective's head snapped round 'Where'? his voice was a harsh whisper.

'Down by the water tower'

Farraday aimed his Night Vision binoculars, in the direction that Monty had indicated, with a nod of his head. When he pressed the focus button, first the water tower loomed into clear sight. Then, as he panned to the left, he saw two black inflatables. For a moment, the racing clouds cleared and the starlight was magnified by the night glasses. The Detective saw eight, black clad figures, fanning out along the shoreline.

'This is what I was afraid of'

'Professionals'? Monty was watching the Policeman closely.

'Yeah'

'Are we going to do what we said'?

'Let's name it for what it is, shall we'! after watching the rapidly moving figures, for a few moments, he continued 'Murder, is what we have in mind'

'You're right. But this isn't simply murder, is it'? he hoped, that it was more than that.

'No it isn't. It's killing for our country'

'Some would even call it, Civil War' Monty mumbled.

'Hmm. Well, in some ways, I suppose it is' Farraday was

watching the dark figures as they stopped, just before they reached the crest, on the river side, of the flood defence. The Detective made ready, to do what he and Monty had spent hours preparing to do. Then he stopped, not able to believe his luck. There was another figure waiting, a little further back, but it was undoubtedly Chief Constable, Dean Wilson. Farraday could not confuse the bulky outline, with that of anyone else 'You'll never guess what'? he could barely conceal his chuckle.

'What'?

'Wilson's here'

'Where'?

'Look' he pointed 'See the figure, holding back'?

'Yes'

'That's him'

'Are you sure'?

'Oh yes'

'So what are you. We. Going to do'? Monty was suddenly overcome, with the enormity of what lay ahead, and what they were hoping to achieve.

'We need to get hold of Wilson. Separate him from his friendly group, of hired killers and then, we need to get him away, somewhere quiet, so that we can get some information out of him, without being interrupted'

'Hector'? Monty tugged at the Detective's sleeve

'They've entered the rushes'

'Ok' Farraday checked to see where Wilson was. He hadn't moved, he was still standing on the same, exact spot 'We'll give them another couple of minutes, then we'll let off the Thunderflashes. With a bit of luck, that'll confuse them enough, to give us time to get hold of Wilson, *and,* get away'

Both men waited. Each, with their own depressing thoughts. Finally, when Farraday spoke, Monty physically jumped.

'Let the party begin' Farraday held a battery in his hand, and checked to make sure that the one wire already connected, to the left terminal, was secure, then, fixed the second wire to the remaining terminal. Finally, after taking a deep breath and a quick glance, in the general direction of Monty, Farraday flicked the switch, that would close the electrical circuit to the Thunderflashes.

Monty and Farraday, both held their breath. Then, after just a few seconds of anguish, the first explosion rent the air, followed almost instantaneously, by a flash of blinding light, that chased the darkness away. In reality, it was impossible to determine which came first. The explosion, or the flash. The initial explosion and flash of blinding light, were quickly followed by others, until the reed bed, was a maelstrom of mind numbing noise and eye scorching light. Small fires had been started by the explosions, and the thick smoke, only served to add to the confusion. The whole thing only lasted for a few minutes, but the angry noise echoed across the fields, like booming thunder.

'**Come on**'! Farraday shouted to Monty, as he jumped up and ran away from the dip in the ground, which had served so well as a hiding place.

Monty ran at full pelt, after the quickly disappearing Detective. Catching up, just in time to see him poke the muzzle of his automatic pistol, into the neck of the Chief Constable.

Wilson had thrown himself to the ground, clamping his hands over his ears, when the first Thunderflash had gone off, staying that way, which made

Farraday's job a lot easier.

'Ok Wilson, get up'

The Chief Constable scrambled to his feet 'What'? he asked, in a shocked voice 'Have you done'? his eyes were wide with fear.

'Just created a bit of a diversion, that's all'

It was then, that they heard the crump, of an exploding Hand Grenade, followed by the scream of an injured man.

Wilson stepped forwards, his fists clenched.

Farraday cocked the hammer on the automatic **'DON'T'**! His warning was simple, but very clear.

'I'll have your balls for earrings. When I've finished with you, nobody will touch you and you'll have nowhere to hide, either'!

'SHUT UP'! Farraday flicked his weapon, in the direction of the water tower 'Walk to the inflatables' Wilson hesitated, and Farraday fired a round into the ground 'The next bullet, has your name on it'

That did the trick. The Chief Constable did as he was told 'Do you know how to use one of these'? Farraday asked Monty.

'I haven't used one for ages, but I suppose that it's like riding a bike'

'Good'! Farraday pointed his gun at Wilson 'Push it into the river'

'Why should I'? Wilson squared his shoulders.

'Because if you don't, I'll drop you were you stand' Wilson chuckled 'You really don't scare me, as far as I'm concerned, you're nothing more than something I've stepped in'! he started to turn away 'And if you think I'm worried, about being shot by you, someone with no back bone'!

Farraday didn't say a word, he just raised his weapon and pulled the trigger.

Chapter Sixty Two

Wilson staggered backwards, his face screwed up in agony, his right hand pressed to his left shoulder. Growling at Farraday, he spoke through clenched teeth, the muscles in his jaw, straining '**You bastard**'! he tried to swallow back, the bile that was rising up from his stomach '**Forget prison. I'll make sure you never get that far**'!

'Oh please. Save it for someone who gives a shit' Farraday flicked the muzzle of his gun, at the rubber boat 'Now push that into the river, and get in' 'But I' : -

'**Just do it**' Farraday was beginning to lose his patience, and was starting to worry about how long they had, before Wilson's heavies turned up.

Wilson struggled to push the inflatable into the retreating tide, just before it started to float, Monty jumped in and went to sit in the stern. Next, Wilson got in, quickly followed by Farraday, who gave the small boat, a shove. Just managing to clamber in, without getting his feet wet. Monty hit the start button, firing up the twin outboard motors, which caught first time. Pushing the throttles forward, Monty turned in a tight arc, heading down stream.

'Where to'? Monty asked.

'Just head for the refinery, and I'll tell you where to go, in a minute'

A whining buzz, made Farraday duck. There had been no sound of gun fire, so he guessed that the sniper was using a silencer. In response, Monty opened the throttles all the way. The boat bucked, as the two powerful engines revved up to full power.

'They'll be coming after us in a moment'! Monty shouted above the wind and the roar of the engines.

'No they won't' Farraday said, as he took aim with his rifle. Dawn was just breaking on the horizon, giving just enough light, for the Detective to see what he was aiming at 'Monty'? he shouted.

'What'?

'Stop'

'Why'? Monty's voice was almost carried away, on the wind.

'I need to get a clear shot'

The boat slowed to a stop, gently rising and falling in the light swell. Farraday took careful aim, timing his shot, so that he was on the crest of a wave, when he fired. As the Detective concentrated on finding the target, Wilson started to inch his way towards him, in the hope that he would be able to tip him over the side. Monty saw what Wilson was doing and took out his automatic pistol. The Chief Constable stopped moving, when he felt the cold muzzle, pressing against the back of his head and heard the metallic click, of the hammer being cocked.

'Stay exactly where you are' Monty chuckled maliciously 'Even I couldn't miss from here'

'Look' Wilson said in a low conspiratorial voice 'We can work something out. You and me'

'Really' Monty answered in a voice, dripping with sarcasm 'I help you get rid of Hector and then what'? his grip on his weapon tightened 'We get to land and at some point, I get a bullet in my brain'!

'I give you my word, that nothing will happen to you'

Monty's laugh was cold 'You expect me to trust you, someone that is a puppet for an illegal operation. As for your, *word*, well that isn't worth diddley squat' 'Listen to me' Wilson's desperation was evident. **'No! You listen to me'**! Monty dug the muzzle of the gun, further into Wilson's neck 'If you want to live long enough to see daylight, then you'd better shut up, because if Hector doesn't shoot you, then *I,* will'! Wilson opened his mouth to argue, but when he saw the shadowed look on Monty's face, he decided against it.

Farraday waited for the next wave crest, took aim and pulled the trigger. The Lee Enfield bucked powerfully against his shoulder. Farraday waited, his breath held, watching to see if his shot was on target. What he saw frustrated him. The bullet went wide of its intended target. Slamming into the brickwork of the old water tower. There was, however, something that disturbed him more. One of the professional killers, was aiming his high powered riffle in their direction. Farraday lifted the bolt and pulled it back, to load a round into the firing chamber, then pushed the bolt back, to its original position. Aiming at the man, he hoped to get a shot of first. As the crosshairs, of the telescopic sight, centred on the chest of the black clad figure, the Policeman squeezed the trigger. He watched as the figure was thrown against the same brickwork, that his first bullet had ricocheted from, then fell forwards, to lay still in the bottom, of one of the other inflatables.

The Detective quickly reloaded. Then fired again at one the outboard motors. This time his aim was true, and he hit what he was firing at.The lead slug, punched a hole in the fuel tank, and petrol started to leak onto the sand.

Looking at Monty, he said 'You'd better get a move on' turning his eyes so that he could see Wilson, he ground his teeth 'I hope you burn in hell, for what you've done' 'You really are a drama queen, aren't you'? his smirk, stretched from one side of his face, to the other.
Farraday stood up, hitting the Chief Constable in the face, with the butt of his rifle.
'**Sit down Hector**'!!! Farraday took a step towards the prone figure, of the senior Policeman '**Hector. Will you sit down**'!!! Monty's voice carried clearly, on the early morning air 'So that I can get going'!
Farraday looked at Monty, then down at Wilson 'Right' he sat down, as he was told.
Monty opened the throttles and the inflatable jumped forward, as it bounced off the next wave top.
'Carry on round the bend in the river, and then you'll see an inlet about a mile along on the left. Go up there as far as you can. Then we can beach the boat'
'What'll happen then. How do we get Wilson to where ever it is, that we're going to take him'?
'We steal a car'
'Are you mad'? Monty was aghast.
'Probably'
'Do you know what'?
'What'? Farraday answered disinterestedly.
'I've spent all my life, doing the right thing'
'Really'? he wasn't surprised.
'Yes, really. And I'll tell you something for nothing'
Monty looked long and hard at Farrday 'I've never, ever, had so much fun' he started to laugh.
It was Farraday's turn to stare 'Let's just hope that you live long enough, to enjoy it fully'
Monty looked at the dour expression of Farraday's face,

and became a little more sober 'Spoil sport' he mumbled.
Farraday was keeping a watchful eye on both Wilson,
and the river behind them, just in case the little group,
that had been sent to cancel him and Monty out, had
managed to catch them up. Wilson lay in the bottom of
the boat, where the spray from the bow wave, had
collected in a small puddle of oily, salt water. Groaning
in pain, his hands covered his bloodied face.
Farraday had no doubt, that he had broken his superiors
nose, and most, if not all, of his front teeth. But he didn't
care. He had spent most of his adult life, fitting against
the evils of, bribery and corruption. He had arrested more
petty criminals and murderers, than he cared to think
about. Wilson wasn't just another criminal, he was much
worse than that. He was one of those, that gave the
orders. One of those, who had the power to make
innocent peoples lives, a living nightmare. And if
Farraday had anything to do with it, then he would make
sure that Wilson, suffered some of his own treatment.
'Over there' he pointed to what looked like a break in the
sea wall.
He followed Farraday's pointing finger 'Ok, I've got it'
Monty turned the inflatable, in a gentle arc. After a few
seconds, he straightened up, heading for the entrance to a
small inlet.
    As they approached the mouth of the creek,
Monty slowed down and both men watched, to make
sure that there was nobody around, to see what they were
doing.
    Just over two hundred yards inland, the creek
ended in a small, soup spoon shaped beech, that was a
mixture of mud and sand. Monty headed towards the
sand, steering the inflatable as high up the beech as

possible, so that they could get out, without getting their feet wet.

'Should we camouflage this thing'? Monty asked, when they where all standing beside it, on the sand.

'No, we've no time'

'So what are we going to do next'?

'Die slowly and painfully. If I have anything to do with it' the Chief Constable mumbled.

Farraday gave Wilson a sharp punch in the kidneys, causing him to collapse to the ground, in a heap.

'I'm going to find us some transport. If he tries to escape, shoot him'!

'It'll be my pleasure' Monty said to Farraday's departing back.

Chapter Sixty Three

Farraday didn't have far to go, before he found
what he was looking for.
The Detective climbed to the top of the sea wall and
looked around. About half a mile to the west, stood an
old farm house. Outside on the large drive, stood three
vehicles. A four wheel drive, a pickup truck and finally, a
battered old saloon. Farraday smiled. The old saloon was
exactly what he was looking for.
Walking up the lane, that would eventually take
him past the entrance to the farm house, he carried on
past the driveway. Farraday had a quick look round,
without making it obvious. Everything was quiet, and he
had seen something else, that would make his task just
that little bit easier. He would be able to use a group of
outhouses, to shield his attempts to steal one of the cars.
Walking along the road, until he was hidden, he came to
a stop. Taking a last, quick, look around, he climbed over
the fence and ran to the side of one of the buildings.
Peering round the corner, he smiled, when he saw that
the way was clear. Strolling to the beat up saloon, as if he
actually lived there, he tried the door handle. When it
opened, he slipped inside.
'Damn' he cursed, when he saw that the keys weren't in
the ignition. Checking the glove compartment, he was
beginning to panic, and he started to rapidly check under
the drivers seat 'At last' placing the key in the ignition,
he didn't stop to think what would happen, when he
started the engine. Surprisingly, the car started first time,

and he pushed the gear shift into first gear. Accelerating away up the drive and into the lane, he couldn't believe his luck, when he looked in the rear view mirror, and saw that the rapidly shrinking house, was devoid of people screaming and shouting at him. Farraday had a kind of inner voice, that would keep chirping every now and then *"That when things were going to well, it usually meant that there was a nasty surprise, sitting just over the horizon, out of site"* today though, he chose to ignore that warning.

Pulling the car to a stop, Farraday ran to the top of the embankment, signaling to Monty to bring Wilson. 'I can't go any further' Wilson moaned.
'Fine' Monty said, as he took the gun from his coat pocket, where it had been hidden, with his fingers wrapped around the handgrip, ready to pull it out at the first sign of trouble 'Die here then'! he cocked the hammer.
'You wouldn't murder a Police officer, surely'? Wilson's eyes were wide with disbelief.
'No, I wouldn't' a cold smile stole over his face 'But I'd put down a mad dog, masquerading as one' he raised the gun, so that it was level with the other man's face.
'Ok, ok' the Policeman turned and started to tramp to the sea wall. A couple of times on his way up the slope, he stumbled and slid back, but neither of his captors offered any help. At last, after about five minutes, he flopped down into the back seat, of the battered car and was almost instantly asleep. The loss of blood and the fear for his life, having brought him to the edge of exhaustion.
'I'm impressed' Farraday slapped Monty on the back.
'Don't be' Monty grimaced 'I was shitting myself'
'I'd never have guessed'

236

Both men got in the car. Monty in the back, with his gun hidden just inside his coat, his hand always firmly gripping it. Farraday getting into the drivers seat.

'Have you any idea, where we're going'? Monty glanced at Wilson, as he asked the Detective his question.

'To the bunker'

Neither of the three men spoke, until they had reached their destination.

Chapter Sixty Four

'What do we do know'? Monty asked.

Both men were standing, looking down at Wilson, who they had placed on an army surplus cot. His wound had been expertly bandaged and didn't appear to be bleeding any more.

'You stay here and keep an eye on him' not that he was going any where, due to the set of handcuffs that were fixed to a metal loop, cemented into one of the walls, and the senior Policeman's right wrist 'And I'll go and ditch the car' as he spoke, he smiled down at his superior 'And then I'll go and find someone, who can prise some answers out of our guest here'

'Oh, and who might that be'? Monty was confused, he thought that they were on their own.

'My friend from the original Commando group, that were acting as bodyguards' Farraday saw the fear in Wilson's eyes, and added 'Unless you want to start telling us the truth now'? Wilson just turned his head away 'Oh well, your choice' patting Monty on the arm, he said 'I could be gone for quite some time'

'Ok' smiling, Monty added 'Be carefull'

'Yes mum' Farraday joked.

Chapter Sixty Five

Farraday had dumped the car that he had stolen, in a ditch, not far from his destination, he couldn't see any point in making his life any harder, than it already was. Now, sitting in the kitchen of the cottage, where the German scientist, Morrela Schlicke, had once lived, he started to wonder about what his plans were.

If Eustace did turn up, and if he could be persuaded to help them, what then? How could he use any of the information gained, to bring the people running this Black Operation, to justice? And if he learned what he learned, how could he use it, to save not only his life, but that of Monty?

It is true of course that, *information is power,* but only if you knew how to use, that information. Farraday looked at his watch. He'd already been waiting for nearly three hours, how much longer should he give it? An hour, two, six?

Almost on cue, the backdoor opened, and Beecher walked in.

'Thought I had company' was all he said, as he dropped his rucksack onto the table, in front of the Policeman.

'You should secure your property better, you never know whose walking around'

The other man simply looked at him, not appreciating his attempt at humour 'What do you want'? he filled a kettle with water and plugged it in. Sitting down opposite the Detective, he waited impatiently for an answer.

Farraday was to tired to play games, so he came right to

the point 'I've got Wilson'

'So why should that interest me'?

'Wilson is one of the leaders, of the group that is after the diaries'

Beecher's interest was evident, by the twinkle in his eyes 'Oh really. And what does this Wilson do then'?

'Chief Constable Wilson' Farraday was pleased at the effect, of what he'd just said, upon the other man. Beecher had been sitting at a slant, his attention shared between the heating water, in the kettle and Farraday. Now however, he turned to face the Detective, full on. All his concentration given over to the Policeman 'So I take it, that he's the government representative'?

'You take it wrong'

'What makes you sat that'? there was no expression on his face, but his eyes were alive and glowed with an inner fire.

'For a start, there was a spy in our camp'

'Who was it'? Beecher's voice was low and gravely.

'Duke. Monty's project manager' Farraday was lost in thought for a moment 'And Wilson was quite happy, to let him be killed, so that he could get at the diaries'

'I see' Beecher shook his head.

'Yeah, and not only that, but he had my boss murdered, because he was threatening to expose their little game'

'That was the Policeman, killed by the car bomb'?

'Yes'

'And you believe that this Wilson, is on the side of the' a smile crossed his face 'The bad guys'?

'Yes I do' the title "Bad guys", was to simple, to innocent, to express what this group of people were capable of, but for the sake of clarity, it would do.

'The trouble is' Beecher frowned 'The line between good

and bad, is so thin, that you'd need an electron microscope to see it'
'But surely it's an easy choice'?
'Why'?
'Because Wilson's crew, wants to profit from the knowledge held in those diaries'
'And you think that our government, would't profit in a similar way'? Beecher's eyes, held those of the Policeman's, neither man looking away.
'Yes. That is, no. I don't think that they would want to'
'Let me put it this way' finally he broke eye contact 'Wilson's group would profit initially, from either selling the information, or, if they have the resources, cloning people and putting them in the right jobs, and using their, *people,* to make them money'
'The government would use the knowledge, to put people in positions of power all over the world. So in time, there would only be one dominant power. That power, would be able to determine what went on, anywhere on the planet. Would you want one man, or woman, running the world'? again he gave Farraday a long hard look 'I know that I wouldn't'
'So, what do I do'?
'Destroy the diaries'
'But they're my only bargaining chip' he was horrified at Beecher's suggestion.
'Do you honestly believe, that your life will be worth, *that*'? he clicked the fingers of his right hand 'Once you hand over, the diaries'?
'I was hoping to find out who the King Pin was, and wipe him out' already he could see major flaws, in his thinking.
'For one thing. Even if you did manage to get him,

someone else would take his place. And for another. The organisation is simply to big. Nobody knows who does what. It's all smoke and mirrors'

'You seem to know an awful lot, for an outsider' Farraday was becoming suspicious.

'That's because I was an insider for many years. Not only for the original group, but also for the new one. That's why I'm determined that those books, shall *never,* get into anyone's hands. Anyone, that is, who can use them'

'What am I going to do with Wilson'? Farraday's head was spinning.

'Let him go'

'But he knows to much'!

'So what are you going to do, kill him'?

'No, of course not'

'Let him go then. He wont be a problem to you'

'Why'? a deep frown creased Farraday's forehead.

'Because he failed in his task, and his bosses don't like failure'

'What will they do with him'? Farraday was curious and surprisingly, a little worried for him.

'That's not your problem' Beecher knew, that once Wilson was let loose, he wouldn't live for more than a few hours. As he'd said. Wilson's superiors, didn't like failure and for any mistake, the operative would pay a high price.

'So'? Farraday said, in a calm voice 'I guess I've no choice' looking at Beecheer, he asked 'Fancy coming to watch a couple of diaries being barbecued'?

'Why not' Beecher answered happily.

Chapter Sixty Six

Farraday waited, while Beecher locked the backdoor to the cottage. Looking around nervously, as he waited for the older man to finish his task.

'There' Beecher gave the door a gentle push 'Should be safe now'

As he turned around, both men heard a quiet pop.Then a hole appeared in the front of Beecher's light coat, followed by a dark, expanding circle of blood.

'Oh' Beecher gasped, as he sank slowly to his knees, before falling forward, to lay face down on the path.

'What'? Farraday mumbled in shock 'Who'? unable to move, he just stood staring down at the prone form of the old Commando.

'It's a pity really' said a female voice, from behind him 'Because, for an old guy, he was really cool'

Farraday looked behind him '**Get him some help**'! his mind was starting to go numb with shock '**Please**'

'No point. My bullet went right through his heart'

'Your bullet'?

'Yes' she took her right hand out from behind her back. Farraday saw the automatic pistol, with the black tube of a silencer, attached, held in the woman's delicate fingers 'Now, why don't we go somewhere quiet, so that we can talk'! it wasn't a question, but an order.

'But what about' : - his voice was quiet, and he sounded slightly drunk.

'Oh, don't worry about him, my friends will sort him out' she smiled cruelly 'I'm sure they'll find somewhere nice, to bury him' a cold laugh, escaped her throat 'A bridge support, or a road, something like that'!

'**You bitch**'! there was little venom in his voice.

'Is that the best that you can do'? she poked him in the ribs, with her gun '**Move**'

'Where too'?

'There's a car in the road. Get in the back'!

Chapter Sixty Seven

The journey was a blur, but Farraday reckoned that they had been driving for about forty minutes, when they slowed and pulled through an old rusty, wire mesh gateway. The Policeman took a look around at his surroundings. The woman not bothering to stop him, what was the point, he wouldn't be leaving here alive. 'What is this place'? Farraday asked, half heartedly. 'It used to be an airfield. One of the Ministry of Defences best kept secrets. Except it didn't hold airplanes, just missiles'
'You're kidding' Farraday's eyes roamed around, trying to see if it was possible, to find any evidence of the airfields past.
'Don't bother looking for clues, everything is under ground' the woman sneered.
'How did they build this place, so near a housing estate, without anybody noticing'?
'They didn't. It used to be all fields around here'
The car that they were travelling in, slowed, before turning into one of the derelict buildings. Finally coming to a stop, in a far corner. The driver got out and opened Farraday's door.
'I take it that the Neanderthal, doesn't speak'?
'**Get out**'! the woman commanded. Farraday just sat looking at her. She looked at the driver, who took this as his cue, to grab hold of the Detective, dumping him unceremoniously on the ground, before standing back 'Are you going to get up, or am I going to have to get

Bruno, to drag you everywhere'?
Farraday looked at the heavy, and smiled 'Bruno, of
course, what else'!
'Are you going to get up'? she was rapidly loosing
patience.
'Ok, ok. Keep your knickers on' Farraday stood up.
The woman nodded in the general direction, of the area
behind the car, where an old dinning chair stood
forlornly. The Policeman did as he was bid.
'**SIT**'! the order was barked, in a cold voice.
'Can I ask a couple of questions, before you beat me to a
pulp'?
'Make it quick'
'What's your name'?
'That's no concern of yours'
'That's a strange name. Is it Welsh'? his feeble attempt at
humour, fell on deaf ears 'Ok' Farraday swallowed 'Did
you kill my colleague'?
'Yes'
The Detective shook his head, as he lowered his eyes, he
looked at the floor 'Poor Steve. He was only just into his
twenties. What a waste'
Bruno took hold of his left arm, forcing it behind the
chair back, he than took Farraday's right arm and did the
same. Finally, taking both of the Detectives wrists, in one
massive hand, he took a set of handcuffs from his right
jacket pocket, clamping one cuff around Farraday's left
wrist, wrapped the linking chain through the back of the
chair, then secured the other end, around his right wrist.
Closing the cuff's so tightly, that the circulation was
nearly cut off from his hands. He didn't struggle, there
was no point, because Bruno was massive. It almost
looked, as if he had been drip fed steroids, from the day

he was born.

Farraday hadn't struggled, but when Bruno stepped around to the front, and stood grinning down at him, the Detective aimed a viscous kick at the other man's groin, which connected perfectly. Bruno never even flinched, he just stepped forward, the enormous blocks, that were his hands, spread wide, ready to grab hold of his victims head, so that he could crush it.

'**NO BRUNO**'! the woman ordered sternly, as if she were talking to a pet dog, who was just about to do something it shouldn't. The disappointment was evident in his eyes 'you can play with him later' Bruno smiled and nodded.

'Doesn't talk much does he'? Farraday was trying hard to conceal his fear. Pleasantly surprised, to hear the defiance in his voice.

'That's because he can't'

'No sense, no feeling' Farraday grinned 'I suppose that's why he didn't react, when I kicked him in the bollo' : -

'That's because he has no testicles' the woman interrupted him 'Years of steroid abuse, made him impotent, so we removed them, to stop them getting in the way'

'Ouch' the Detective grimaced 'Or not, as the case may be'

'Roll up his sleeve'

Bruno did as he was told, except he didn't roll up Farraday's shirt sleeve, he simply ripped it off.

'Hey. This is my favourite shirt'! Farraday shouted at the heavy.

'We can do this the easy way' again, that cold, heartless smile 'Or, and this is my favourite, we can do it the hard way' she hoped that it would be the later, as she liked nothing more, than causing people, especially men, excruciating pain.

'What, you ask me a question, and if I refuse to answer, you get ape man to rough me up'?

'Oh no. We don't do things like that now' she bent forward, running the fingernail, of her right index finger, over Farraday's right eye, which he quickly screwed shut 'We only do that sort of thing, for fun' she stepped back 'What we use now, are these' she held up a metal case, that must have been hidden somewhere close by.

Farraday watched as she handed the attache sized case, to Bruno, who rested it on the palms of his hands. The woman un-clipped the locks, and after lifting the lid, showed him the bottles inside, nestling beside a selection of hyperdermic needles and syringes 'Do you like my portable cocktail cabinet'? when Farraday didn't answer, she continued 'All the best people have them, you know' she ran her fingers lovingly over the contents.

Farraday finally found hid voice 'What, you actually carry Sodium Pentathol, around with you'?

She shook her head 'Oh no, that stuff is so last decade' she smiled 'These little gems, can make you have your worst nightmares all in one go, *and*, while you're still awake. They can paralyse you, make your nerve endings feel like they're being microwaved, from the inside. Oh, and so much more' then, pointing to the last bottle on the left, she said 'And this baby, is my favourite' she took it out and kissed it 'This causes your body temperature to go so high, that you literally cook in your own juices' she laughed 'I actually had the pleasure, of watching this one work'

'Oh, how lovely for you' Farraday had been trying to break the bar, on the back his seat, but it was proving to

248

be far to tough for him.

The woman shook herself from the reverie, she had fallen into 'But today, I'll use this one' she took a syringe from its holder and pushed the needle through the seal, at the top of one of the small bottles. Pulling the plunger, she filled the syringe to the second line, with a bluish liquid 'It'll loosen your tongue in no time'

As she came near Farraday, he lashed out with his right leg, managing to get a lucky strike, which hit her behind her knees. Instantly she went down and Farraday jumped up, giving her a good solid kick, under the chin.

Bruno may have been big and powerful, but he was slow to react. Standing still, confusion acting like heavy weights on his nervous system, his sluggish brain struggling with what to do. Which move should he make first? he stood motionless. The woman groaned. Farraday had been hindered by the chair, and his kick had lacked its full power.

'**OYE**'! the Detective called to Bruno, who turned his eyes slowly to look at him 'No nuts' Bruno's lips pulled back over his teeth, in a noiseless snarl 'What's the matter. Can't you think for yourself'? the heavy took a faltering step forward 'To afraid that you won't be able to handle me, without some help from your little girl friend'? Farraday was bent over, because of the chair, that he was having to hold with both handcuffed hands. If he got this wrong, then he was going to die, a very painful death 'Where's your balls? Oh sorry, I forgot, you ain't got none'

That was it, Bruno couldn't hold back his anger any longer. With two massive strides, he was in front of Farraday. Picking the Policeman up by the front of his shirt, he gave him a series of neck breaking shakes, before quite literally, throwing him, as if he were no more than a rag doll, against the nearest wall. Farraday hit the brickwork, sideways on, with a bone jarring crash, that, because his hands were anchored behind him, his shoulders were forced into a vulnerable position. The policeman howled in pain, as his left shoulder popped out of its socket, and he and the chair, to which he was fixed, fell to the floor. Bruno was at his side a few seconds later. Bending down, he picked up the groaning Policeman. This time using the chair, he power lifted Farraday and threw him again. Playing with him, like a cat plays with a mouse, before it finally puts it out of its misery. Farraday hit the floor with a jolt, that knocked the air out of his lungs. But more importantly, for the Policeman at least, one of the front legs landed first. The chair splintered, and with the full weight of Farraday, coming to rest on it, finally broke. The fact that his arms were now free, escaped his stunned brain. As his assailant moved in, in the hope of inflicting even more damage, Farraday realised that his arms were no longer tethered, and managed to get his feet between his spread hands, the chain that joined the handcuffs, just long enough, although not long enough to prevent fiery pain, from shooting down his left arm, from his injured shoulder.

Standing up, Farraday was just in time to sidestep Bruno's attack, with only one good arm, he knew that he would need something to even the odds. Looking around, his eyes came to rest on the syringe, that lay near the woman's fingers. Rushing to her side, he just had time to pick up the metal object and turn to face his attacker. The man mountain, started to wrap his arms around Farraday's upper body, the muscles of his upper limbs, like thick steel rope. Just in time, the Detective got his right arm free, from the other man's crushing embrace. Bruno's breath blasted in foul waves, straight into his face, Farraday turned his head away, in the hope that he could breath in some fresh air.

The heavy, squeezed harder. Farraday felt his ribs grate together. He knew that he didn't have long, as the edges of his vision had started to blur. So with the last of his strength, he plunged the needle into Bruno's back, pushing the plunger all the way in.

At first nothing happened. Then suddenly, Bruno's arms dropped and he staggered back. Finally falling to his knees, his muscles went slack, and he slid sideways, until he lay still, on the floor.

Farraday stood staring down at Bruno, as he lay on the ground, unable to move. The only part of his body that seemed to be working, were his eyes, and they stared back at the Detective, with hate filled anger. The Policeman searched through the bodyguards pockets, until he found what he was looking for. With a jangle, the keys to the handcuffs, came free from one of Bruno's trousers pockets. Quickly, he released himself and then turned. What he saw first, was the muzzle of an automatic, just a few inches away from his face and pointing between his eyes.

Chapter Sixty Eight

'I'll give you one thing' Farraday said in a cold voice,
full of frustration 'You're a lot tougher than you look'
'Give me one reason, why I shouldn't kill you right
now'?
'Because my mother loves me' the woman clicked off the
safety catch, her finger tightened on the trigger 'And
because there's a man over there' his head nodded just
once, to the right. His eyes never leaving hers 'Who has
you firmly in the sights, of a high powered riffle'
'You really think I'm stupid enough, to fall for that old
trick'?
The bullet, that she never knew was coming, hit her in
the left temple, exploding in a red jelly cloud, from the
right side of her head. Her dead body, slumped to the
ground, as the welcoming arms of death, came and took
her into its land of eternal darkness.

'I thought that you were dead'? Farraday said, in a
happy, surprised voice.
'It'll take more than a single bullet, to kill me'
'I don't understand, how you could still be alive. That
bullet must have hit you in the heart'?
'Well, if I were a, *normal,* person, I would be dead. But
I'm one of their earlier specimens, and my heart is on the
right side'
'You're kiding' Farraday was about to laugh, but he felt
that it might be discourteous, so he simply smiled.
'No' it was Beecher's turn to smile 'I was one of the first

252

experiments, and somehow my heart ended up in the wrong place. I never thought that one day, it would save my life'

'Or mine' Farrday said, in a low voice.

'What happens now'? Beecher asked.

'I'm not sure'

'You still have the diaries'?

'Yes' Farraday nodded.

'Destroy them'!

'But they're all the hard evidence I have' again Farraday was shocked by Beecher's advice.

'All the time they're still around, there's the chance that someone will get their hands on them, and this whole mery-go-round, will start again'

'So what do we do. Sorry. What do I do, about Wilson'?

'Turn him in, to the authorities. Let them worry about it' he smiled coldly 'And you never know, his bosses might save the tax paying public, some money, by arranging for him to have an accident'

'I can't do that'

'What, turn him in'?

'No. Turn him in, so that he can be' the word stuck in his throat 'Murdered'

'Why not, he'd do the same to you'? he put his hand on Farraday's shoulder.

'Doesn't make it right' Farraday was starting to fidget, he wanted to get going.

'Wilson used people, and when they had come to the end of their usefulness, he made them disappear'

'How come you know so much'? Farraday was, again, becoming suspicious.

'I told you, I was an insider' he looked at the Policeman, his head held high and his chin stuck out.

253

'Oh yeah'

'I was one of them. But' the memories made his head spin 'But'

'What'?

'I became to old, and rather than take the risk, that I might blab, they tried to have me killed' anger flashed in his eyes and echoed in his words 'Me, their faithful servant of over sixty years. When it came down to it, I was nothing more than a commodity, to be used and then thrown away'

'Aren't we all'?

'Yeah, but when you get to the end of your useful career, your bosses don't put a contract out on your head'

'I'm not sure that, that's true at this point in my career'

'Hmm' Beecher considered, that Farraday could be right.

'Ok'! Farraday said decisively.

'Ok. What'?

'I'll do what you suggested' it went against the grain to hand over the reins, but this thing was far to big for him to handle.

'Good. Why don't you call on this, and I'll disappear' he turned to walk away.

Farraday grabbed him 'No you don't'

Beecher looked at the Detective's hand and then up at the man himself 'I have no choice, I can't be found'

'But how do I explain this'? he looked around.

'Oh, I'm sure you'll think of something' an ingratiating smile, was plastered on his face.

'Looks like I have no choice'

Chapter Sixty Nine

The old Home Guard weapons dump, was crawling with Police and Secret Service officers. They were going over every inch of the site, to see if they could learn anything. Farraday had already told them, that there was no need for them to search the underground store. But they simply ignored him. Their refusal to listen to him, made him, not only paranoid but extremely suspicious.

'Excuse me' Farraday walked over to the suit in charge.

'Detective Sergeant Farraday, how may I help you'? he looked at the Policeman for a second, and then back at the open trap door.

'I'm afraid that you have me at a disadvantage'

'Oh, and why's that'?

'I don't know your name'

'Hmm' the suited man smiled 'Digger. Just call me Digger'

'Is that it'?

'Yes'

'Ok then, Digger' Farraday stopped speaking, until he had Digger's full attention 'I went over every inch of that place, and I found nothing'

'But I take it, that you hid the diaries there'? his eyes glinted with an internal light, almost as if he were playing cat and mouse with the Detective, and Farraday was the mouse.

'Yes, I told you. And Mr. Barrington-Wright, was there protecting them, and, holding Chief Constable Wilson, for safe keeping'

'Really'! Digger smiled coldly 'Next time you choose someone, to do the job of jailer, I suggest you pick someone better qualified, than Mr. Barrington-Wright'

'Why. I don't understand'? confusion rocked his mind.

'When we got here, we found your man on the floor unconscious, and, Wilson was gone'

'Shit'

'Yes, exactly'

'Is Monty' he corrected himself 'Mr. Barrington-Wright, ok'? concern clouded his eyes.

'Apart from a big bump on his head, and a bad headache, he's fine'

Farraday nodded his head 'So what now'?

'We've taken over, and we shall be investigating all those involved' his eyes took on a distant look 'It would appear that this thing, this corruption, has spread further than we thought possible'

'I know. It's in the Police force and, in the world of high finance. Surely it can't have gone much further'?

Farraday still held out a little hope.

Digger, almost laughed at Farraday's naivety 'This thing has got its claws, into the Military, the Secret Security Forces and even, the high ranks of the government'

Farraday was shocked 'And if those diaries get into the wrong hands, then who knows what could happen'?

'Looks like they already have'

'W, what do you mean'?

'The diaries that you refer to, are no longer in their hiding place'

'Oh no' the Detective shook his head, before placing it in his hands 'So after all we've been through, and all the people that have died, I've still failed'

Digger patted him on the back 'Why don't you go home and get some rest. You look done in'? his face and eyes, reflected his compassion.

Farraday nodded dumbly 'I think I'll do that'

'And remember' Digger said in a voice full of sincerity 'You did more than anyone else, could ever have done'!

'Thanks' Farraday mumbled, as he walked slowly back to his car.

Chapter Seventy

Over the weeks that followed, a massive investigation took place. Bigger, some people said, than this country had ever seen before.

Farraday was questioned for hours on end, the same things were asked, time and time again, over and over, until he could recite the questions and answers in his sleep. Which, he was told, was something he did frequently. Of course, Detective Sergeant Farraday, was cleared of any wrong doing. He was even commended for his professionalism and honesty. Even so, he was left feeling dirty, almost as if he had been touched by something unclean, that had left a rotten stench, that hung around him like a shroud.

Steve Lucas's body, was never found. The only people that could possibly throw any light on the subject, were either dead, or had gone into deep hiding. Farraday felt as if something had been left unresolved. He put this down to the fact, that he truly felt, that until Steve Lucas's body had been found and laid to rest, he would never be able to close this chapter of his life, and he would forever feel, just that little bit unfinished.

One thing experience had taught him, was that if you were patient enough, and looked in the right place, you'd get the information that you were waiting for. That information came to him, as he sat in his car, waiting for the lights to change. He had taken two weeks off, then gone back to work, putting what had happened to the back of his mind, not that he'd had any choice, everything had been taken out of his hands.

'Hello Detective Sergeant Farraday' Digger said, as he made himself comfortable, in the front passenger seat. Farraday sat looking at his passenger, not noticing that the traffic lights had turned green. Only turning his attention back to the road, when the driver behind him gave an angry, impatient honk of his car horn. Neither man said anything, until Farraday had found somewhere safe to park. The delay, having giving the Detective a chance to find his voice.

'This is an unexpected surprise' he had been expecting some sort of visit, due to the fact that his enquiries, had been met with an uneasy silence.

'Hmm' Digger said, as he turned his attention away from the street, looking back at Farraday 'You must have been expecting it'? his face was neutral, his tone conversational.

'Sort of'

'Well I guess, I don't blame you, after all that happened to you' he searched the other mans face, before saying 'I'm going to tell you, what you want to know. Well, most of it, anyway'

'Really'? Farrday was suddenly suspicious.

'But there are two provisos'!

'Go on'

'One. You never breath a word of what I tell you. Two. You stop trying to investigate this case. And that includes, stopping any and, *all,* questions'

'Right' this was the best he could hope for. Better in fact, than he had dared, hope for.

'I have your word'? his face had become serious, and his voice had deepened slightly.

'You do' Farraday nodded his head, adding weight to his conviction.

'But just so we understand each other, I'll tell you this. If you *ever*, break you word, even by the smallest amount, I'll have you killed. Do I make myself clear'?

'Yeah' Farraday suddenly felt very uneasy, and gave the fact away, by licking his lips.

'Ok' Digger smiled, but it was cold, without a hint of humour, or humanity 'This' he struggled with a name to call what had happened 'Situation' he settled for that bland word 'This attempt to continue the earlier work of Ghosting, wasn't exactly unknown to us' Farraday gasped. The noise just an inrush of air, but it carried a great weight of expectation 'No' shaking his head sadly, he continued 'We've known about it for sometime. We were hoping, that they would carry on with the experiments, so that when, if, they were successful, we could step in and take over. Our government could then use the process, for their own purposes. Should they choose to do so'

'Who are, *they*'? Farraday asked, as his anger rose.

'*They,* are a group of industrialists, financiers and politicians'

'And you let them go on'?

'Yup'

'Even though it could be potentially disastrous, for the rest of the world. *If*, the information fell into the wrong hands'?

'Yes' Digger dabbed the sweat beading on his forehead, with a white handkerchief 'But things are never that simple'

'Of course they are. All you had to do' : - Farraday was cut dead.

'Do you want to learn more, or not'? it was Digger's turn to show anger.

'You know I do'

'Shut up then'! the suited agent waited for Farraday to make a comment. But none came 'A view was taken, that it would be better, if we had the ability to clone people, because then, *we,* would be able to develop a means to detect a clone. That was the theory, anyway' he shook his head 'Somehow, the group in charge of the private laboratories, got wind of our scheme and over night, they simply disappeared. It took us years to find them, but by then, they were so far advanced, that we were almost to late'

'You said, *almost*'?

'Yes, because they needed some vital information to finish their work'

'And that information, was held in Doctor Schlicke's diaries'

'It was'

'And without it, they were unable to complete their experiments'? Farraday smiled inwardly.

'For the time being, anyway'

'Are you always so pessimistic'?

Finally Digger smiled 'It's part of the job'

'I know what you mean'

'Anyway' the Secret Service man looked at his watch 'With the help of our man Beecher' : -

'Beecher'?

'Yeah'

'He was working for you'? Farraday was incredulous.

'Uh huh'

'For how long'?

'A few years. But that's not important now' he waited for

a couple of seconds, before carrying on 'We started to close in, and that's when the proverbial, hit the fan. They started to get itchy trigger fingers, and people started to die' after rubbing his face in both hands, he turned to look at Farraday 'Some were innocent, some were not'
'Why were so many people killed'?
'Up until that point, the people in charge had been happy to take a softly, softly, approach. Go into peoples houses and not be seen. But that takes time, something that they obviously felt, they had very little of'
'And so, because they felt that they were being squeezed, they became sloppy'
'I guess so. Not loosing their invisibility, became second on their list of priorities'
'Are you any closer to finding, who was, is, in charge'?
'Oh yes' Digger's face held a satisfied smile 'We've made about eleven arrests'
'Wow' Farraday was also pleased.
'And with the evidence that they gave, voluntarily or not' he said cryptically 'We're about to make some more'
'Can you give me any names'? not that it mattered, Farraday was just curious.
'NO'! Digger smiled 'But I can say, that they vary in rank, within the government and the governments various departments'
'Does that include the Security Services'?
'Oh yes. And if you keep an eye on the news, you'll see a lot of changes announced'
'Did you find Wilson'?
'We did'
'Was he dead'?
'No. He was very much alive and willing to talk'
'Good' Farraday wasn't quite sure what he meant, by that

one word. *Good*, that he didn't get away. Or *good*, that
he wasn't another one of the fatalities.
'Strange thing though'?
'What is'?
Digger glanced sideways at the Policeman, watching for
any tell tale signs 'He told us, that he never found the
diaries'
'Really'? Farraday looked suitably disturbed 'So do you
believe him, and if you do, who could possibly have
them'?
'I believe him alright! And to answer your second
question. I have my suspicions'
'And whom do you suspect'?
Digger tapped the side of his nose 'I just hope, that who
ever has them, decides to destroy them. Because, all the
time that they are out there, in the big wide world, they
pose a very real threat'
'How do you know, that this person, or persons, won't
sell them'?
'Because, if I'm right, and I hope to high heaven, I am.
Then I think that this person, has only one interest in
mind'
'What's that then'?
'The safety of his country' Digger opened the car door,
he put one foot out onto the pavement, before turning
back to face Farraday 'I'm sure that out paths will cross
again'
The passenger door slammed shut, and Farraday's
unexpected guest, was lost in the passing hordes.

Chapter Seventy One

The next few months, saw some very high profile government figures, disappear from public life. In some cases, they not only departed from view, but also from the intimate circles in which they travelled. Farraday noticed one other thing, that also stood out, and that was the press. They had become strangely quiet.

It was evident, to Farraday at least, that they had been silenced. Something that was not exactly easy, in a society that believed in the *freedom of the press.*

Farraday still mourned the loss of D. C. Steve Lucas, and for a while, he was unsure of what to do. Stay with the force, or leave? In the end, he decided to stay. After all, what else would he do? Nothing else would measure up to, *the job,* he truly loved. But even so, he did change. Nothing felt as secure, as it once had and with that feeling of change, came a belief that, life was for living, and never again, would he take it for granted.

The moon was just a feint glow in the sky, as Farraday looked around to make sure that he wasn't being watched. Off in the distance a fox barked, grating on his nerve endings, causing him to flinch, almost as if the sound would somehow, warn someone of his presence in the meadow. Giving himself a shake, the Detective took a package out of the bag, he had carried with him, and put it down on the ground. After taking a torch from his jacket, he worked quickly by its shaded light. Carefully, he dug up a turf, about twelve inches square, and placed it to the side. Removing the soil, to a depth of nearly three feet, before, with a sigh, he decided that he was happy with what he had done. Placing the oil cloth wrapped package, back in the canvas bag, Faraday looked around again, and once he was happy, set the bundle in the bottom of the hole and then, filled it in. Finally, he replaced the turf, then stamped it down. Standing up, he cleaned the spade with his left hand, then he walked to his car.

    With a last quick glance at his surroundings, Farraday got into his car and just as the sun came into view over the horizon, put his key in the ignition and gave it a twist.

Chapter Seventy Two

For the first time in days, Detective Sergeant Hector Farraday, was able to sit down and watch the evening news. With a mug of strong tea in one hand, and a bacon sandwich in the other, he watched as the first story started to unfold. Nothing very exciting, just more scenes of the Prime Minister, meeting various dignitaries from around the world.

The thing that struck Farraday the most, was how young the Prime Minister looked. It was amazing, just a few weeks ago, he was starting to look old and haggard. But now, he looked almost half his age and not a wrinkle in site, well hardly a wrinkle. *"I wonder how he does it"*. Suddenly, he found himself starting to wonder. *"No, they couldn't have"?* as he started to ponder, the why's and the wherefores, his heart started to race. *"Best not go down that road"*. His mind called to him and with a grunt, he turned the television off.

Chapter Seventy Three

      The Prime Minister looked at his reflection in the mirror, marvelling at just how young he looked. There was hardly a blemish, or the merest hint of any crows feet in sight. His youthful looks, bellied his fifty years, and he knew that, had he not have been in the public eye, he could have passed himself off as a much younger man. 'Oh' he chuckled to himself 'The wonders of modern science'

The End

(Or is it?)